The Gallows of Heaven

The Gallows of Heaven

I.O. Adler

Lucas Ross Publishing

Contents

The Gallows of Heaven
by
I.O. Adler
Old Chrome Book Four

Copyright © 2022 I.O. Adler

All rights reserved. No part of this publication may be reproduced, stored in a retrieval system, copied in any form or by any means, electronic, mechanical, photocopying, or recording, or otherwise transmitted without written permission from the publisher. You must not circulate this book in any format.

Published by Lucas Ross Publishing.

Edited by Dave Pasquantonio, www.davepasquantonio.com

Author website: ioadler.com

This is a work of fiction. Names, characters, places, brands, media, and incidents are either the product of the author's imagination or are used fictitiously. Any resemblance to similarly named places or to persons living or deceased is unintentional.

Chapter One

Santabutra Sin had a lead on Miles Kim, and he couldn't catch her. Could barely keep up. The sun was almost directly above them and felt like it was leaning particularly close that late morning. A stitch ran down his side and his breathing came ragged.

His dog darted past, clipping his leg and threatening to send him toppling to the dirt. It dove into a row of thistles and flushed a family of quail, which flew in every direction. But the dog was too distracted to pursue any of the fleeing birds. The animal sniffed about spastically and appeared intent on a patch of stones where a lizard had taken shelter.

"Leave it," Miles ordered.

He had to repeat himself before the dog responded by bounding on ahead of him. His dog. His *robot* dog. Indistinguishable, except for a close inspection that would uncover the truth, including a bar code and recessed access panels, so the owner, in this case Miles, could empty the contents of its stomach in case it ate anything. No owner found, even after he had posted about a lost animal on Seraph net.

Up ahead, Santabutra climbed to the top of a rock and perched at the edge. She glanced in his direction and gave a big wave. He grimaced and waved back before finishing the climb, joining her at the top and trying hard not to pass out.

"It's...really hot," he said.

"Boo-hoo. Would have been cooler if we would have started when I said."

"I got held up."

"Buying one of your junkie neighbors breakfast isn't going to change their lot in life."

"You never know. One good day might be all it takes."

"I've seen your neighbors."

The view from the crest of the plateau took in the hills and expansive desert plains to the north, with the sprawl of Seraph behind them. A layer of lavender clouds clung low on the western horizon, but the threat of rain was off the table, as the sky had been clearing since dawn.

Miles fought to get comfortable on the hard stone. "Neighbor's name is Hatima. He turns tricks most nights but lost his card key after getting robbed."

"And how many other neighbors like him need your help today? You've got to get a better apartment."

The dog barked a few times at nothing before sniffing about the base of their rock.

"Sorry, that was cynical," she added. "This view is worth the exertion, isn't it?"

"How often do you do this?"

"Three times a week with my running partners. But we don't stop like this. Just listen."

"I don't hear anything—"

"Shh."

While his ear implant wasn't especially keen, he could make out the faint reverse beeper of some unseen piece of heavy machinery from down below, along with an electrical hum coming off a transformer near the communication towers past the crest.

"It's not perfect, is it?" she asked finally.

"The silence? Beats being down in the city. River City army base was like that, too. Never quiet."

"Hell is loud noises. You should try coming here early. But you'll need to be in better shape."

He peered over the lip of the boulder. "Use it or lose it, right? Or lose it and have it bolted back onto you. Can't believe you run this. Told you I'd slow you down. Dragging me here was your idea."

"Relax, Miles. I'm having fun. But it's also cooler earlier in the day. Today isn't bad for the sleeping-in crowd. You wanted to do something with me that didn't cost money, so here we are."

"I didn't think lung replacements were cheap."

She grinned. "You're just out of shape, old man."

They began the walk downhill. Santabutra hadn't broken a sweat, while Miles mopped his brow and his shirt kept clinging to his skin. The dog once again raced ahead of them, taking point and hurriedly sniffing many of the same spots he had inspected on their climb up.

She waited at a smooth slope as if worrying he might slip. "This is your last day off, unless you changed your mind about the job. I can't believe you said yes."

"I've got to eat."

"Don't we all? But you've done your duty. Security job's still waiting for you with your buddy Tristan, isn't it?"

"I've got my medical bills. They were more than I expected."

"You mean from Doctor Brook? The guy who almost killed your friend Dawn, shot two Red Banner militia, and would have sold you for parts?"

It was true. But Doctor Brook had eventually helped him when they were confronted by the Meridian agents hot on the trail of the IFF transponder. And Miles' right hand was as good as new after the repairs performed at the doctor's clinic. Even now, Doctor Brook was in jail awaiting sentencing. His clinic had somehow found Miles on Seraph net and had sent three past due statements for services rendered.

"I told Barma I'd come on board," Miles said. "He's short-handed. I've got experience."

"Can't help it, can you? You're abused by the notion that you can make a difference."

"Seraph's my home now. Of course I can do some good. Why do *you* do it?"

"Don't get defensive. I'm still off active duty. I thought I'd hate riding a desk, but it has its benefits. Not having to take calls after hours is one of them. Having my mornings is another. Time for lunch? There's a new noodle shop near the Yellow Tiger HQ."

"Can't. Need time to shower and change. Then Marshal Barma wants me to check in this afternoon for orientation."

She chuckled. "Orientation. Knowing him, it's going to be a pat on the head and a push out the door."

"Maybe. He promised to show me the ropes."

"Last time I checked, the marshals didn't exactly have a field manual to study."

"Figured as much. But I don't want to be late. He also told me to pack an overnight bag."

Chapter Two

"You're late."

Marshal Barma sat wedged at his desk, typing away at a terminal. His hand cannon sat atop a stack of papers, along with a teacup that had already put several wet rings on the documents.

Miles placed his bag on the floor and took a chair opposite Barma. "You said two o'clock."

"And I texted you to change it to noon. I have forms for you to fill out. We can do this on paper or electronically."

"Electronic is fine."

The marshal waved at a tablet covered by a folder. Miles took it. Waiting for him was a lengthy employment application, a liability release form, a DPA for medical decisions in case of incapacitation, an intent in case of death letter, a confidentiality agreement, a no-hostage policy statement, a conduct code, and about twenty more pages that required a virtual date and signature.

He got hung up on the first page.

Barma glanced at him. "Have your robot brain do it for you, if you want to show off. That'll save time."

"I prefer to make things harder on myself. It's asking for my name."

"You forget already?"

"I'm wanted. Putting my real name down doesn't sound like a good idea."

"Let me worry about that. Make something up if you have to. Add a middle initial. That'll throw them off."

Miles couldn't tell if the marshal was serious. He left his name blank and filled out everything else he could, hoping his address at the hotel counted as a legal residence. While the dive had marginally improved under the new manager, it was still loud, uncomfortable, and possibly dangerous. Plus, the manager didn't like the dog.

Glenda, the marshal's assistant, was leaning on her desk, feeding blueberries to his robot animal. "Aren't you the cutie pie?" The hound was up on his haunches, snapping up each treat and barking in anticipation of the next.

Barma hadn't yet commented on the animal. When Miles made it to the bottom of the last form, Barma waved for him to hand the tablet over. "That bag all you're taking?"

"You haven't exactly told me anything. Figured I'd need a toothbrush and change of underwear for my locker here."

"Uh-uh. You're on the road. So find a kennel for your animal."

"Okay. Where are we going?"

"Not we. You and Marshal Jodie. You'll be gone a week."

"A week?"

"Yeah. What, did you think, you'd be sitting at a desk? That's the job. We go out past Seraph limits and remind everyone that they're civilized. It's in the service documentation, if you're forgetting what we do."

Miles had uploaded it but hadn't read it through.

"Problem with that?" Barma asked. When Miles shook his head, Barma continued, his tone softening. "I'd like nothing more than to ease you in. We've lost contact with a couple of marshals in the last month. Our budget doesn't support sending us out in twos, but I don't have a choice."

"I guess an increase in budget isn't in the cards."

"Sheriff Vaca is pushing hard to have all our duties subsumed by Red District and dissolve our office, leaving a token marshal in place who would never leave city hall. We have a relationship with the communities outside of Seraph that won't be replaced by any by-the-hour rent-a-soldiers driving their tanks. Herron-Cauley is looking to expand, which means a third police force. And Mayor Bedford is actually considering it. In the meantime, we do our job. For you, it means on-the-road training."

"I thought you'd be the one showing me the ropes."

"Marshal Jodie is a good man. A bit twitchy, but who isn't these days? He's old like you, so take his advice with a grain of salt. He's a little blind, but not bad enough to affect his work. On the plus side, he knows the territory better than anyone."

"Can't wait to meet him."

Barma nodded agreeably. "And he's looking forward to working with you. He's out back right now with your ride. Fair warning: he'll insist on driving."

***

Marshal Jodie was lean with a medium build, his broad hat hardly concealing his thin, gray hair. He wore a tan leather duster, a wrinkled sepia checkered button-down shirt, and a badge clipped to a chest pocket. Stubble peppered his chin and mouth, and his nose and cheeks were richly lined with swollen blood vessels.

"Barma hired another old hand," Jodie said. "Ha-ha. Looks like we'll be stuck together for a spell. Not sure I agree with two marshals on duty together. Cover more territory on my own, but he's the boss, right?"

Miles clung to the loop handle above the passenger side door as their desert runner raced past the light traffic on the southern road. Behind them, in the small space beneath the hatch, the dog sat with his head up, intent on the passing scenery. The animal puffed his mouth whenever they passed someone on the side of the road, but never barked. Jodie hadn't complained, and Miles didn't want to spring for kennel fees.

At a Y intersection, Marshal Jodie took the dirt track rather than keep to the wide, paved lane that would bring them westward through scattered farms and towards the distant trading post linking Seraph with Pacific City. His foot never left the accelerator.

"You'll probably notice a difference in style between Barma and me," Jodie continued. "See, I'm a light touch. Barma? Heavy handed. Part of the new breed. No patience. Folks respond better to a marshal who doesn't throw his weight around. You've worked with Barma. You know what I'm talking about."

Miles couldn't tell if this was a joke about Barma's size. "Yeah, I worked with him some."

An eruption of dirt and gravel beneath the vehicle proved jarring as they left the smooth road behind them at a sign reading "Now Leaving Seraph."

Miles had been this way once before when chasing after Agatha Fish. But a couple of hours into this drive, with the late afternoon sun threatening to vanish behind low clouds, he confirmed with Insight that they were indeed in unfamiliar territory.

Jodie drove straight over a series of deep ruts, the suspension barely keeping up. Miles gritted his teeth to keep from biting his tongue. The runner handled it well enough and appeared to be outfitted for rough terrain, with spare battery, extra tires, and a winch.

"Where are we going?" Miles asked. "Do you have a route?"

"I play it by ear. Every camp and settlement should be checked on at least once a month. Some need more attention. It's all spinning platters, see? Keep each going, let them all feel the love, make sure they see my face, knock a few heads, and that's the work week."

Miles tried to track their location.

No network available, Insight said.

"What settlement are we heading for? My map's not up."

"Map's not much use out here if you're hoping for Seraph net to show in your augment. So relax, we keep in contact with radio. Looks like you packed light. We sometimes need to sleep rough, but don't worry; I have an extra bedroll, and Glenda packed some lunches. But pro tip? If you value your teeth and your morning constitutionals, you'll bring your own victuals."

The lane grew narrow as it passed through a canyon with high sandstone walls on either side. If another vehicle were to come their way, it would be a tight fit. They came to another intersection, and Jodie didn't pause as he took the left road. Another fork fifteen minutes later, and he took a right. Even smaller and fainter tracks ran off in several directions. The dog was curled up now and barely taking notice of the landscape.

Miles scanned the roadside for any signs but saw none. "You either know where you're going or you're getting us lost."

"Some locals like to cut down the signs. Think it keeps them independent. Once you've driven this a few dozen times, you'll know it like the backside of your hand."

He pulled them onto a flat patch of ground a dozen meters off the road and parked. Thick reeds grew clumped at the opposite side of some boulders. A small stream trickled past. Once out of the vehicle, a quick inspection confirmed they were alone, but there was an old fire ring of rock. The dog made a careful inspection with purpose, his nose now a dusty gray.

"First camp's another hour or so off," Jodie said. "Considering our late start, this spot will do. I wouldn't drink the water, but it's good for washing up."

"Wouldn't the settlement be a safer place to sleep?"

"Didn't Barma tell you anything before partnering us up? There's a reason the folks out here want nothing to do with Seraph. The law's one of them. While there are a few places we can get a room, that settlement isn't one of them." He pulled two rolls out of the runner's rear compartment. "You want lumpy or extra lumpy?"

Chapter Three

Miles' phone signal clung to fifteen percent. When Dillan answered, his son's voice cut out.

"—that you? ...hear me?"

"Dillan, it's dad. I'm just checking in."

"—can barely hear you. Where are you?"

"I took that job with Marshal Barma. I'm on a patrol and it's going to have me out of signal range for a few days, so I thought I'd say hi before that happens."

"Just heading out..." Dillan said before breaking up.

Miles checked his device. Still connected, but the signal was at 8%.

"Don't know if you can still hear me. Just wanted to wish you and Zoe a good morning, and I'll call you tomorrow if I get the chance."

Either Dillan hung up or the connection faded to zero.

8:15 a.m. Miles put the device away. The dog was staring up at him expectantly. Marshal Jodie had packed his bedroll and sleeping bag while a propane stove boiled water. He poured tea in a carafe and dropped in a handful of loose-leaf tea, setting it aside to let it steep. More water went into a bowl where Jodie emptied a small bag of cereal, which smelled bready and beer-like.

Jodie motioned with the empty bag. "Got extra packets, if you want."

The dog had moved to Jodie's side and nudged him.

"I've got half my sandwich," Miles said. "I'm fine."

"Suit yourself. Might not have time later to cook lunch. How about that dog of yours? Haven't seen you feed him."

The robot dog didn't need food. And if someone gave it any, it would need to be cleaned out, like the blueberries from the previous day. Most people didn't realize it was an artificial animal, including Miles, up until Santabutra had pointed it out.

Jodie lowered a spoonful of porridge. The dog gobbled it up. "Once we have our tea, we'll get going. Day's driving ahead of us, and it feels like it's going to be a hot one."

***

Late morning, and they were speeding across a stretch of hardpan. The sun was bright on the dirty windshield, and Miles had a hard time seeing through a cloud of dust.

A six-wheel buggy raced before them. Miles zoomed in. The corner of one fender bore the Yellow Tiger logo. The buggy weaved around the rocks and clusters of acacia. They were climbing in elevation, approaching a high hill with sheer cliffs. The dog leaned forward, ears up, intent on the vehicle they were pursuing. The buggy took a track barely wide enough for its fat tires.

Marshal Jodie didn't hesitate to follow, leaning on the horn. "Pull that rig over!" he shouted over the runner's loudspeaker. But the buggy didn't slow even as it crested the ridge path and bounded over a line of jagged rocks. When the runner struck the obstacle, the sharp jolt of the vehicle's bottom hitting unyielding stone felt like the car was going to crack wide open.

Barma's voice crackled over the radio. "You have him?" *Crackle.* "...have him. Can't..." *Crackle-crackle.* "Reading me?"

"Do not copy, chief," Jodie said. "Repeat, do not copy. But we're in pursuit."

"Suspect is..." The rest of Barma's call vanished in the static.

Miles checked his burner before sliding it back into his shoulder holster. They followed the buggy up a winding trail along the top of the ridge. They were heading for a series of broken rocks that neither vehicle could cross unless they sprouted wings.

Jodie grinned. "Gotcha!"

It was impossible to see the buggy in the rising wave of chalky dust.

Then their runner hit something. The collision caused the vehicle to lurch upward and spin out before landing back down on its tires. Red lights blinked from the dash. Jodie kept gunning the engine, but the engine had quit.

"Stay," Miles ordered the dog. He unclipped the seatbelt harness and climbed out, dropping for cover and waiting for the bank of dust to settle. Jodie let out a slew of curses as he fumbled with his own restraints before unceremoniously tumbling out of the car, which teetered atop a lump of rock beneath the chassis.

Jodie took a moment to get his balance before straightening his hat. "Hey, jackass!" he shouted at the Yellow Tiger buggy. "Show your hands and get over here now!"

"Stay down," Miles hissed.

"Nonsense. Whoever's driving that thing knows when they're licked."

Jodie marched forward. Miles hesitated for a second before joining him, his eyes scanning the haze for any signs of movement.

The buggy had its rearmost tires off the ground. It had collided straight on into a set of boulders. The driver's side gull door stood open. Deployed airbags lay deflated on the driver's seat. No driver, and no one hiding behind the vehicle.

"Seriously?" Jodie said. "It's too hot for this. Too hot! Hey, jackass—"

Miles grabbed his arm. "Keep low. He might be armed."

"Yeah, maybe. But if they start shooting, we get to shoot back. Barma said you're loaded to the gills with combat mods."

"I don't have combat modifications. Insight can target lock, but with all this dust, our burners are useless."

"That's your first mistake. Burners are toys for pimps and a show for spit-and-polish militia brats. You want people out here to respect you, bring a real gun."

As if to underscore the comment, Jodie cleared a long-barrel pistol from a thigh holster. Past the buggy was a gap in the boulders. Jodie took the lead, squeezing through to an uneven path that climbed ever upward.

Miles looked for a way where they could split up but found none. With rocks above and all around them, even a lone defender could ambush them both with little effort. He kept his weapon raised and eyes moving.

"You stole that car. We caught you fair and square," Jodie shouted. "Looks like you're hung up. You don't want us to abandon you all the way up here, do you?" When no answer came, Jodie chambered a round in his weapon. "Hard way it is, then."

A spatter of blood on the rock. Miles pointed to it, but Jodie kept walking.

Miles stopped him. Whispered, "Hold up. He's hurt."

"That'll make this easier."

"Why would someone steal a Yellow Tiger vehicle?"

"I've stopped trying to understand the criminal mind. Are we done? It's hot out, and I want to catch this guy."

"He's down a vehicle, on foot, and injured. He won't get far. Let me try."

Jodie motioned for Miles to walk ahead of him. "Suit yourself."

"Cover me."

Miles inched forward to where the rock passage opened wide. A graveled slope ran down to a shaded gully with a black pool of water. Plenty of boulders to hide behind. A formation of crumbling rock stood above it. At the crest, gnarled trees with a smattering of anemic yellow leaves rose from the tortured ground as if skeletal fingers reaching into the sky.

"This is Deputy Marshal Kim," Miles said loudly. "I know you're hurt. I want to help you get out of here alive."

He slid down a section of loose shale. Scanned the ground. Another few blood drops near a jagged outcropping. He let out a sharp exhale before getting closer. Miles was exposed. If the perp was armed, he'd have a perfect shot.

"My gun's put away. We're not Yellow Tiger. We're with the marshals, and this is your best opportunity to walk out of this in one piece. I can get you medical help."

Feet were visible on the ground. Miles edged closer. The car thief was lying on his side and wearing soft footwear, like slippers, and lime green pants. A pale young man with a sunburned face. He had his arm curled against his chest and wrapped in a blood-soaked rag. The green pants were part of a jumpsuit all the same color. He raised his good hand to shield the sunlight from his eyes. Blinked and smiled.

"Good Sir Marshal, we meet again."

Chapter Four

"Paxton Walker? What are you doing out here?"

Miles had last seen the young man during a train trip from River City. He had been a prisoner of Marshal Barma.

Walker straightened the front of the jumpsuit. Beach Farm was stenciled in black, along with the number 145978.

"You escaped from jail?" Miles asked.

"A dramatic pause in my rehabilitation, I assure you." He struggled to sit up. "Extant circumstances within the facility forced my hand."

Marshal Jodie hurried over. "You got him."

Miles crouched and patted Walker down. "Carrying anything I need to worry about?"

"Perhaps my current circumstances would be different if I did. Seems I upset some of my fellow jailbirds. Flight was my only option."

"Search him good," Jodie said.

"I assure you I'm unarmed," Walker continued. "I was relying on the goodwill of the facility officers as surety against violence. Alas, it seems not all specimens of peace officers are as upright as you exemplary members of the marshal service, and the convicts who are intent on harm are practiced in the arts of influence peddling."

Miles got Walker to his feet and gave him a second frisking before Jodie placed cuffs on his wrists. The rag on Walker's arm was covered in both old and new bloodstains. A long gash ran down the skin and oozed red. It would need stitches, but he'd live.

"Long way back," Miles said to Jodie. "We have a two-seater."

"May I offer a suggestion?" Walker said.

Jodie was on his device. "No signal."

"You've retrieved the misappropriated conveyance. Take it. I promise I've been properly adjusted by my time in Seraph's house of correction."

"Shut up," Miles said. "What's our usual play here?"

Jodie fussed some more before putting the phone away. "Usually I don't have a passenger. When things are complicated, I call Glenda for a pickup, and she sends a wagon. Sometimes she drives out herself if it's close, but most often she sends for a Red District car. But their patrols don't normally make it this far out. Suppose we could clear the back hatch space. Would mean a bumpy ride, but he'll survive. Hope the dog doesn't bite."

Miles checked his own device. No service.

"Tower down, maybe," Jodie said.

Walker raised his cuffed hands. "If I may? While contemplating how best to convey your most cooperative detainee back to his deserved place of incarceration, may I get a drink at yon watering hole? All this excitement has dried my throat."

Miles led him down to the shaded pool. "Make it quick."

Walker kneeled and lapped up water with both hands. Miles crouched and washed up before scooping up a palmful of water. Froze.

Someone lay at the opposite bank of the pool in the darkest shadows.

Miles let the water drain between his fingers. "Stop drinking."

When Walker looked up, he spewed out the contents of his mouth and scrambled away from the edge of the pool. Jodie had his phone held aloft and hadn't noticed.

"Jodie." Miles rose and approached the prone figure. It wasn't moving. It was a man, perhaps in his early forties, bearded, dark hair, wearing pants with patched knees and suspenders. His shirt was unbuttoned and loose, with an undershirt that had once been white but was dark with brown soil stains. His eyes were open and rolled back. White crust lined his mouth and nostrils. His swollen tongue stuck partway out between his lips. The body was bloated.

"What have you got there, Kim?" Jodie called.

Walker was still on the ground, wide eyed and wiping at his mouth. "It's the water, isn't it? He was poisoned!"

Miles got closer to the body. "Calm down. We don't know."

He checked the man's neck for a pulse before scanning the nearby ground. Then he went through the man's pockets. Some were already turned inside out. No wallet or ID, but in a small front belt pouch he found a pair of coins and an empty wrapper of pills from a medicine printer. He set the coins aside and examined the dead man's wrists. The skin appeared frayed and discolored from what might have been bruising, but the body's condition made it hard to know for sure.

"We need a forensic bot or a tech here," Miles said.

Jodie crouched next to him. "Yeah, not going to happen. No signal, so no way to call. The hard truth of it is, I've seen this sort of thing."

"What are you talking about?"

"Fellow gets lost out here and succumbs to the elements. Sun, heat, no supplies."

"He didn't starve, and there's water here," Miles said.

"He got lucky, but not soon enough. Baked brain, hypothermia...sips from the pool won't stop that. I'll mark it, and we get one of the locals to come out and take care of the corpse. In the meantime, we cover him up ourselves. It's the decent thing."

"That's a lot of guessing there. Look at his wrists. He was tied up."

"Hard to say what happened. We can take some pictures. But we've got a fugitive to get to lockup."

Paxton Walker coughed and spat.

Miles got a better look at the dead man's swollen face. "Be good to know who this was."

"Then go back to the runner. We have a sample kit. Get hair and a skin scraping. We'll check it with our network once we're back in signal range, but don't hold your breath on results. Seraph folks don't want to be in anyone's database, and people out in the barrens even more so."

"What about the body?"

Jodie walked up a ways from the pool and inspected the area. "This spot's as good as any. All right, Walker. Grab that stiff and drag him up here, then we'll pile some rocks on top of him. Step lively. It's going to be hot, and we don't want to end up like him, do we?"

Chapter Five

"This thing isn't going anywhere."

Marshal Jodie took a step back from the stolen Yellow Tiger buggy. Something beneath the vehicle was leaking. An axle was cracked, and two of the six tires were canted at an odd angle.

"Suppose we could remove the two tires, leaves us four," he continued, "and we use it to cart Walker back home, and you can drive our runner."

Miles used Insight to review the scene where they had found the dead man next to the spring. They had missed nothing obvious. Perhaps it was as Jodie said and the man had died of exposure. Paxton Walker stood sullenly by as Jodie circled the disabled vehicle. The sun was directly overhead, and true to Jodie's proclamation, the heat weighed down on them.

"Marshal Kim," Jodie was saying. "You paying attention? I said bring the runner over and set up the winch."

Miles cleared his vision of the images. "Looks like there are some metal parts dragging. Taking tires off isn't going to get this rig running over this terrain."

"Whelp, looks like we're squeezing into ours, then. Walker, prepare to get comfortable."

As Jodie took the prisoner back to the runner, Miles inspected the buggy's interior. The cargo space behind the front seats was empty. Dried blood marked the upholstery of the driver's seat. A key card stuck out of the ignition slot. Miles checked the power. The console lit up, displaying the engine charge and other vitals, the system oblivious to the damage to the chassis. He tapped the screen. A navigation map appeared.

No network, the system flashed.

But there was a map function, and the buggy was parked on top of a pinned waypoint.

Miles moved the map to show more of the surrounding area. The pin remained in place. The only other item of interest was a green spot labeled Manna. He pulled the key and pocketed it, the power winking off. A first aid kit was clipped beneath the dash next to an empty weapon rack.

Marshal Jodie had their runner's rear hatch open and was pulling out the jack and the spare tire. The dog was out and circulating about Miles' and their fugitive's legs. Walker kept his cuffed hands up and didn't appear to know what to do about the animal.

Jodie tossed the jack down to the ground next to the tire. "Figure without these, we can make him fit."

Miles pushed Walker against the side of the runner. "You picked this spot on your map, didn't you?"

Walker licked his lips. "Why, Sir Marshal, I don't know what you're talking about."

"You had it selected on your navigation screen. That dead man...who was he?"

"I don't know him. I was escaping my confines because I was afraid for my life."

"You say you want to be cooperative? Who were you meeting, Walker? Because someone else made it to your rendezvous and might have been looking for you. This third party might still be out here somewhere."

"I don't know this desert, and I wasn't meeting anyone."

Miles studied the man's face before stepping back. "If you say so. But this is too much of a coincidence. We have you. You're going back whether or not you cooperate. Cooperation makes this mess go easier for you. So if you know anything, this is the time to share."

Walker blinked several times. "When I say I wasn't meeting anyone, dear marshal, I mean I had a contact and a handle of the person I had engaged. 'Foxglove,' a nom de guerre, I assure you. I didn't even have a description. I know nothing about him or her. When I messaged them, they said they'd be waiting for me here and would have paperwork, ID, and would help me get to New Pacific."

"Why not drive there yourself? I thought New Pacific took anyone."

"Seraph isn't the only town where I am less than welcome."

Miles studied the fugitive. "So you break out of jail in Seraph, steal a runner, and drive out to the middle of nowhere. How were you planning on paying this Foxglove person?"

"I had promised credits. I would have delivered, too, if my fellow inmates had been less astute. Shame on me for trusting a fellow scofflaw. They weren't supposed to spot my double dealing until I made my escape. I am, as they say, broke."

Marshal Jodie had been listening. "Well, you better think about a better story than that if you intend to smooth things over with your fellow inmates. Because you're going back."

Walker sounded wistful. "I thought the militia vehicle might have served as compensation for my contact's services. I could have been on my way to a new start, a fresh beginning. Good marshals, you know I can't return to prison. The others will kill me. Look at my arm. They almost did already."

"You should have thought of that before conning more people. Now get in the car."

The dog preceded Walker into the back and watched with interest as Walker climbed tentatively in beside him. They both had to scoot down as the hatch closed.

"This is inhumane," Walker said.

Marshal Jodie double checked the hatch was shut before coming around to climb in behind the steering wheel. "Shut your yap. The dog's not complaining."

Miles got comfortable in the passenger seat as Jodie jammed the start button over and over. The engine made no sound. He took the key card in and out and pressed the button a few more times. Wiped the card clean and blew on it before reinserting it.

No dashboard lights. Miles tried the compartment light, but it didn't work.

He got out and inspected the runner. Popped the hood. While his wife Seo Yeun had been the mechanic, he had picked up enough to know what was right and what was wrong in an engine compartment. The melted and blackened plugs and cables running out of the car's computer were his first clues. The palm-sized box of circuitry appeared to have been knocked off its crumbling mount and had been resting on the power converter. Heat and friction had done the rest, and their trip across the bumpy terrain had finished the job. Rust and gunk marked the engine.

"Well, Kim?" Jodie called.

"We're not going anywhere with the runner."

Jodie joined him under the hood. "What happened?"

"Rough driving. Computer's shot. Look at the corrosion. It's a wonder the runner made it this far."

"I keep telling Barma we need to switch to horses, not that they're much cheaper."

"Do we not have a maintenance staff?"

"Why do you think Barma drives his own car? We're not as well funded as the militias. Welcome to the marshal service."

Miles had a few questions that went unasked. Hadn't Jodie noticed any warning lights during their drive? Had he checked the vehicle over before they had set out? It had been a daily routine in the Meridian military.

Still no signal on the device. He checked the runner's radio. It wouldn't power up.

"We have tools?" Miles asked. "I can rewire the radio directly to the battery pack."

Jodie got Walker and the dog out of the back. In the recessed tire compartment, a hollow space marked where a toolkit might have once been found.

Walker looked back and forth between the marshals. "What does this mean?"

Jodie slapped him hard on the shoulder. "It means I hope those shoes are comfortable. We're walking."

Chapter Six

They drank from the pool. Miles took a moment to drizzle water on his face. Marshal Jodie used a bottle and chugged down as much as he could. Walker waited and watched before taking his fill as the afternoon heat settled heavy on top of the ridge.

The body was now under a pile of rocks. Miles wasn't sure of what animals roamed the desert, but if they might preserve the body for a later investigation, it was worth the effort. He took the time to search the rest of the area. Besides the odd trees high above them, there was little else of interest.

He searched for boot prints or tire tracks, or even a hidden vehicle. How had Walker's contact arrived there? But the ridge was vast, with too many locations where a bike or car might be concealed. Miles counted a dozen or more places that could lead to a trail to descend the ridge but decided exploring and climbing back up would take time and effort. They couldn't stay there much longer, and they'd need light to walk.

Miles led the way, with Jodie escorting Walker, who remained cuffed and shuffled along as best he could, with the soft prison slippers offering his feet little protection from the jagged rocks. The dog, for once, wasn't running ahead of them, having his own issues in navigating the treacherous ground.

Jodie kept up a stream of talk. "You in the service, Kim? Knocks me out of first place as oldest marshal. Glenda can't wait for her retirement and when she heard Barma was taking a war vet on, she had a few things to say on the subject. 'Course, I wouldn't presume to say it for her. 'But why would a fellow who barely knows the town jump in like that with both feet?' she said. 'Stirring up the pot with the Fishes and Sheriff Vaca. Everyone runs out of luck one day.' And she's right. Eventually, we have our final ride."

Miles was half listening. The last thing he needed was to twist an ankle. If any of them got hurt, it meant trouble. And if Walker's contact Foxglove had been murdered, whoever did it might be out there and watching from any number of vantage points.

They were heading for what appeared to be a trail at the base of a slope of shale. Sure enough, there were traces of old tracks, either quad bikes or motorcycles, vehicles with narrow wheelbases smaller than their out-of-commission desert runner.

"What's near here?" Miles asked.

"Suppose it would be good to know I'm not just walking us around in circles, eh? Small camp not too far off. Haven't visited it in a while. And when I say small, I mean, how do these sand grubbers survive? Place called Manna. Should make it by dusk if Walker here doesn't tarry."

Walker wasn't moving fast. Jodie gave him a shove, and Walker almost fell. But he got up without complaint, and they continued their downhill trudge.

Near the bottom of the slope, the dog took off. It made a beeline for what appeared to be a pile of debris on a shaded landing. Miles followed.

It was a collapsed tent. Near it was a smashed radio handset. Consumer grade, cheap plastic case. According to Insight, the small radio had a range of twenty kilometers under ideal circumstances. A quick check of the grounds found nothing else. The tent appeared to have been cut open, and the rods that once held it up were broken.

A damp patch near a rock looked like a good amount of water or liquid had been dumped out. A tire track marked the ground. A bicycle or small motorcycle, Miles guessed. But there was no way to know which direction they had gone.

"What you got there, Kim?" Jodie called.

Miles examined the tent, but it was empty. "Someone didn't like their camping equipment. Doesn't make sense, busting the radio. Seems like something that could be useful out here."

"Maybe this Foxglove did this."

"Or Foxglove set up camp and whoever got him did this in search of something. What do you know about him, Walker?"

"Very little, I'm afraid," Walker said. "I trusted in his good faith to perform his task. And I imagine he would have followed through if he hadn't been waylaid."

Miles got the dog by the collar. "We still don't know what happened to him."

Neither of the other men contradicted him.

***

Marshal Jodie was sucking on a dry blade of grass. "My last partner, he was something. He would go on and on. Story after story, each wilder and stranger. Shootout with a gang of Metal Heads and the sole survivor. Poisoned by a lizard. A lizard. Can you imagine? Hit by lightning. Had two drug pusher suspects both outdraw him at the Seraph Return Day carnival. Both had dead batteries in their burners, and he put them in the ground. When he paused between stories, I always said it was because of writer's block."

Miles did his best to focus on each step, his feet sore, his muscles aching, sweat dribbling down his body. "What happened to your partner?"

"Heart attack a few years back."

The sun was vanishing, but the heat radiated from the ground.

At least they were following a track. Hardly a road, but there were ruts and more signs of treaded wheels having passed that way, and it was mostly flat and free of the sharp rocks that had been the constant feature of their hike down the ridge.

The dog walked next to him, mirroring his exhaustion. What inside of the thing was causing it to act this way? Did he have a charge running low? Or was this part of a behavior program that mimicked what a real animal might do under the circumstances? Whatever the reason, it made him feel a little better not being the only one who looked ready to drop.

Walker stopped to adjust one of his shoes. It had torn along its seam and was barely keeping together. Jodie didn't shove him this time, appearing content to wait.

Miles caught a whiff of smoke. The trail ahead widened, and beyond lay a broad vale between sandstone cliffs where a collection of prefab homes lined the road to either side. Large tents and makeshift shanties occupied several terraces, connected by cut paths and stairs of wood and a swaying bridge of rope.

A hazy glow radiated from the camp.

"Manna," a painted sign read. One of the posts was cracked and sagged.

Jodie gave Walker a nudge. "The happiest place south of Seraph. Watch your dog here, Kim. The locals are mighty lean."

People stared at them from the cover of their porches. Tarps, sheet metal, and scrap composites made up the makeshift overhangs, but some appeared well-crafted and adorned with decorative ribbons, vines, scraps of wood, and feathers.

Miles gave a nod to a bushy-browed crone who didn't return the gesture. A dog on a long rope came bounding at them, barking and snapping. Miles' dog retreated to his legs, tail down and ears drooping.

"Butch Elder was the camp strong man," Jodie said. "He used to have a radio."

One of a few larger buildings had a generator humming outside, with wires running to its neighbors. Solar panels covered the rooftops. Through a set of open doors came bright lights and violin music. The fiddler stood in one corner, a foot on a chair, a bowler hat canted back. They didn't miss a beat as Miles, Jodie, and Walker entered.

There were several other patrons sitting in two groups. The conversations stopped.

A plank set on stacked crates served as a bar. A young girl in a wheelchair waited expectantly as they approached. She grabbed for a bottle and three shot glasses and paid no mind as the dog sniffed the floor near her.

"How about some waters?" Miles asked.

The girl made a face, then took a pitcher from the back counter and got glasses. "You have coin?"

Miles took out his wallet and produced a credit chip.

"I said coin."

Marshal Jodie leaned a fist on the bar. "You're in Seraph territory. You take credits. And what's a little girl like you doing running this place?"

The bartender pivoted her chair and jutted her jaw forward. "Dad said no credits, so no credits."

The marshal pointed his forefinger. "You folks want to do commerce in Seraph, then you take the credits. Unless, of course, the water and drinks are on the house."

Miles placed a placating hand on the marshal's shoulder. "What's wrong with credits?" he asked the girl.

"No net, no way to know if the credits are good," she said. "Too many hucksters."

"Then how do we get coin?"

"Buy, sell, trade, or steal," a new voice said.

A woman in a long gray dress and a white pinafore stood from one table and approached them. Her black hair was neatly tied behind her head. She had intense green eyes and wore a warm yet bemused expression. "Give them water, Tanni. But drink will cost coin. It's only fair. Don't matter if you're law or not."

Jodie opened his duster and showed the badge on his shirt. "We have credits and they'll spend here."

The woman's mouth tightened. The patrons at the two tables whispered and watched.

Miles fished out the coins he had taken from the dead man. "We have coin. What's your name?"

"Jayakarta. Jaya's fine."

"Is this enough for water?"

"It's more than enough. Tanni, make sure you give them change."

Tanni lined up three glasses of water.

Paxton Walker offered Jaya his hand. "Paxton Walker the Fourth.

Indisposed, but at your service. Please don't mind the adornments on my wrist. They in no way speak to my character."

Marshal Jodie clamped a hand on Walker's neck and brought him to the bar. "Drink your water. And then we're leaving."

Walker took a moment to compose himself before inspecting the glass. From the look on his face, he didn't like what he saw. "I don't suppose I could have a shot of the mescal."

"What brings you here so late?" Jaya asked Miles.

"Car trouble. Is there a radio available?"

"That depends on who you ask. None here in camp. Some think the Alcotts have one, but it could be rumor. And you don't want to deal with them if you don't have to."

"You probably noticed that I'm new here," Miles said. "Who are the Alcotts?"

"Wait around here long enough, and you'll find out. You'll have to excuse me. My prayer group is finished for the evening, and it's sundown."

"What happens at sundown?"

"Here? Not much if you're lucky, marshal. I'll put in a word for you."

She rejoined her table. The group linked hands, and a soft prayer began. The tension broken, the other patrons' attention returned to their drinks.

Miles smelled the contents of his glass and drank. Had worse. He finished it, set the glass down, and pointed to it, giving Tanni a winning smile. She gave him a refill.

He turned to Jodie. "Jaya told me someone named the Alcotts had a radio."

"Two genetically enhanced sisters with a small crew," Jodie said. "Real names unknown. Go by Dora and Ruthie. Local muscle, they keep out of Seraph, so usually there's no problem with them."

"You know where they live?"

"Here in Manna. But I don't want to spend a minute more than I have to here. Sit on Walker while I go and find us transportation."

"You have money I don't know about?" Miles asked.

"I didn't say anything about *buying* a ride."

The marshal exited through the door. After a chorus of amens, Jaya and her group rose, taking time to push in the chairs before likewise departing. A few other customers filtered out. It left one table of drinkers who passed a bottle around and weren't using glasses. One of them gestured to Tanni, who wheeled around the edge of the bar and brought them another bottle for a coin.

"Your friend we found from here?" Miles asked Walker.

Walker had helped himself to more water and took a seat at the recently vacated table. He began examining one of his feet. "New Pacific."

"Yeah, you mentioned he was going to take you there. But this is the closest community to the spring. Chance that someone here did something to him."

"We didn't exchange pleasantries, marshal. As much as this hamlet is delightful, I don't believe anyone comes here to stay. Those that do don't leave."

Tanni returned behind the bar. She pulled a device out from a canvas bag strapped to the back of the wheelchair and began reading.

"Can you answer some questions?" Miles asked her.

Tanni shrugged without looking up.

"Is there a doctor in Manna?"

"You don't look sick."

Miles tried his best to smile pleasantly. "I'm not."

"You met her. Not a real doc, but Jayakarta's the one they call."

"How about if someone died?"

Tanni raised an eyebrow. "Did someone die?"

Miles realized he needed to be careful. He didn't know these people, the camp, or the region. If Paxton Walker's contact hadn't died of natural causes, the camp might be harboring a murderer.

"Just trying to understand the area and to know what resources are here."

"Because that's your job, right? Drive through once every couple of months so you can tax us?"

"You're probably right. Every couple of months isn't very often, is it? I imagine it's hard living out here. But it doesn't look that bad."

"It's a garbage hole. Are you going to order something else?"

"You have the last of the coin. So what do you do for school?"

Her irritable look would have caused a lesser man to shrink back.

"You can't keep bar all day, every day, can you?" he pressed.

"Oh, if only the Seraph child services would come and rescue me from my life in bondage to my cruel taskmaster," she said scornfully. "Please. My dad says to talk nice to the customers. But seeing as you're broke…. Is there anything else you want?"

"Yeah. One more question. Know anyone who goes by the name Foxglove?"

She shook her head and went back to her tablet. Walker had his jail slippers off. They were shredded. His feet were a mass of dirty abrasions and cuts. An older man and woman entered the bar and joined the table of drinkers. The woman waved Tanni over, and they purchased another bottle.

Miles went to the door to peer outside. The sun had set, and the last red clouds were fading to a deeper purple. A few of the brighter stars shone down. Some of the nearby homes had lights, but most of Manna was pitch black. No sign of Marshal Jodie. He returned to sit with Walker.

"Will the marshal service be providing evening victuals?" Walker asked. "Or is it to be death by starvation?"

Before Miles could answer, a man ducked in from the flap behind the bar. He whispered a few words to Tanni, who immediately wheeled herself out through the back. The man was mostly bald with thick curly hair around the sides. He wore a leather vest with no shirt to hide his hairy chest and stomach. The drawstring on his loose pants appeared frayed and ready to give way. The man, the bar owner Miles guessed, made a show of wiping down and tried hard not to look at Miles or Walker.

Then a colossal woman appeared at the front door. Tall and muscular were understatements. She had to stoop down to get past the doorframe, and when she stood erect, her topknot almost brushed the ceiling. Plastic armor adorned her chest, abdomen, and shoulders, but each piece was too small, almost decorative with how much it left unprotected. The remnants of a howling dragon decal in mid snarl embellished one shoulder.

Insight flagged the faded markings on the armor. *Special Assault Fifth Squadron. Ice Dragons. Meridian Corporation.*

She held a short-barrel shotgun casually in one hand, the weapon like a toy. She looked straight at Miles. "Someone claiming to be a marshal in here? There's no law in Manna. Not unless you're me."

Chapter Seven

The giant walked straight towards Miles. Walker stumbled from his chair to get out of the way. Miles rose and backed up to the bar, Insight momentarily blocking his vision with tentative targeting squares. He kept his hand away from his burner as she leaned in.

"I hear you're causing problems, marshal," she said. The word "marshal" had a distinct slur. The large woman's face was flushed. "Problems...in *my* town."

Miles had a hand up. "No problems. We're on a patrol and not looking to upset anyone. Can I buy you a drink?"

"This is my place. I don't need you trying to spend worthless Seraph credits here."

He felt a droplet of spittle strike his eye. "You have me confused with Marshal Jodie. We cleared that up and purchased our water with coin. I'd love to sit down and have a word with you, Ms...."

The shotgun swung back and forth in her left hand. "You're a Metal Head."

"I'm a Seraph deputy marshal. We're here because our vehicle broke down."

"You're not alone."

Miles wasn't sure if it was a question. "Like I said, Marshal Jodie and I came together, along with a fugitive we apprehended. Your name? Is it Alcott?"

She glanced at Walker as if just noticing him. "Dora."

When Dora Alcott moved, it was fast. Insight and his gun hand might have beaten her to the punch, drawn, and fired, if he hadn't dismissed the targeting. She gripped him by his shirt and pressed him back against the bar. When he drew his burner, she knocked it aside with the shotgun. The bartender removed a dirty glass from the bar and stood back.

Her breath smelled of warm onions. "There's...two of you?"

The weight of her fist pressing on his chest made breathing difficult. "I'm Marshal Kim. Marshal Jodie's with me. Here to serve."

Walker approached her. "If I may? The good marshal isn't here for any business in Manna but to bring me to justice. I'm Paxton Walker the Fourth. You and your sister's reputation is well known to me. It's an honor."

"Never heard of you," Dora grunted.

"Surely the case. We came only to find respite, a drink, and perhaps a way for these fine lawgivers to call their office. A radio, perhaps?"

"And you're their prisoner?"

He showed the cuffs. "Alas. So if you wish these men out of your business, a radio will expedite—"

She smacked him with the shotgun, sending him tumbling into the chairs and down to the floor. "Talk too much."

"Let go of the marshal, Dora," Marshal Jodie said as he entered the bar with his long barrel pistol raised.

Dora moved the shotgun so it pressed against Miles' throat. "Since when do marshals hire Metal Heads?"

"Not a Metal Head," Miles gasped.

Jodie moved closer, the gun steady. "Don't make me splatter your brains across the back of the bar."

She appeared to be considering the options. Her face scrunched, as if trying to remember something. Another giant appeared behind the bartender. She was larger than Dora by a few inches, with a mane of red hair that had a life of its own. Insight was too distracted for an accurate height measurement, busily reminding Miles that his target was too close to safely use his firearm, despite the fact the woman was threatening to break his neck.

"Dora!" the second giant shouted.

She let Miles go. Miles gripped the bar to prevent himself from falling as he sucked sweet oxygen into his lungs.

Jodie kept the weapon aimed but lowered it to his hip. "Hello, Ruthie."

Ruthie Alcott wore a thin tank top and a knee-length skirt. Her massive frame stretched both garments to the limit. Blue inks covered her arms, chest, and legs. Her voice was scratchy as if she had been doing too much shouting. "Marshal Jodie. Heard you were in camp. Thought you rode alone."

"Thought I'd bring reinforcements this time."

Ruthie moved to help her sister to a bench on one side of the tent and got her seated. "You don't have anything to worry about here. We're law-abiding citizens."

"Looks like Dora was assaulting a fellow marshal."

"I'm fine," Miles said. His chest ached where Dora's hand had been pressing.

"He shouldn't have come in here unannounced. You know how she gets. So is this going to be a thing?"

Jodie glanced at Miles. Miles straightened his shirt and recovered his burner. Nodded. Walker was getting up and took a chair. He appeared woozy, but otherwise only had a red mark on one cheek.

Marshal Jodie holstered the weapon. "No permanent harm done."

"Thought he was a Metal Head," Dora grumbled.

Her sister brought her a glass of water. Watched her drink. Gave her a pill from a tiny bag and waited for her to swallow. After taking the glass away, she set it on the bar and faced Miles and Jodie.

"How can we help you marshals?"

"A radio would be a good start," Jodie said.

"Tower's down. Went out a week ago. Was back up for a few hours yesterday, then out again. Sent a tech out this morning and didn't hear back yet. So no radio. Head north. Maybe Footsteps from Limbo or The Place Where We Buried Gail?"

"Car broke down," Miles said.

Jodie nodded. "Manna was the closest camp."

Ruthie Alcott got under one of her sister's arms. "I'm going to put Dora to bed. Best if you three left camp."

"Why Ruthie Alcott, what kind of hospitality is this? It's too dark for us to just go stumbling around. You know that. Is there a vehicle here we can borrow?"

"Not likely. My tech has ours. There are a couple horses, some motorbikes, but they belong to people who use them."

"That means we're staying."

Ruthie had her sister leaning on her. "All right, marshals, looks like you three are guests, whether or not I like it. I'll see you squared away for the night. But don't expect to be comfortable."

Chapter Eight

The canvas tent let a breeze in. It would have been pleasant during the day, but the night chill reached through the canvas walls like icy hands, and the sleeping bag on Miles' cot looked too short for an adult.

The barkeep had guided them to their accommodations. A pitcher of water and a platter of cold tamales served as supper. They had sat and eaten in silence after the man had departed, his last words lingering.

"Best stay in the tent tonight, and don't leave."

A small chemical toilet waited for them right outside the flap. The tent was one of several on a terrace away from the main road. Moving shadows at the nearby hovels, along with the sounds of voices, whispers mostly, were the only signs of life from their neighbors.

Manna, at least this night, turned in early.

Their tent had four cots in total and a trunk with old clothes. An electric lamp hanging from a hook on a tent pole threw out orange light. Everything smelled dusty, and a faint aroma of mint vape clung to the bedrolls. The dog whined nervously as he curled up beneath Miles' cot.

"Ruthie Alcott is in charge of the camp?" Miles asked Jodie.

"Yeah. She is now, so it appears."

"She was less than pleasant."

"We've got a place to rest our head."

"We're exposed here," Miles said. "And she said it would be best if we left. That's a passive threat if I ever heard one."

Jodie shifted where he sat on his cot. Shirt off, he was wiping himself down with a damp cloth. "I know. You get a few hours' sleep and then take over for me. One of us stays awake for anyone looking to make trouble, and when the sun rises, we get out of this place. I'll be outside."

"You think someone will try something?"

"Don't you? You saw the Alcott sisters. Enough rough characters drift through these camps. It's always best to expect the worst."

Miles flattened out the sleeping bag to see if it might stretch. "I would have suggested it if you hadn't." He found a zipper and pulled the bag open. Decided it would work best as a wrap. "Walking out of here won't be easy with Walker's feet in the shape they're in. And I don't enjoy leaving the body where we left it."

"This isn't Seraph. Nothing's going to happen to it. We deliver Walker, we come back and work the scene. But it's like I said: he got drunk and wandered off. The desert doesn't suffer fools."

"A lot can happen in the few days it will take to return. An option would be for you to take Walker and leave me, assuming we find a ride. I'll go back to the spring and take a second look around, make sure no one messes with the body."

Jodie buttoned up his shirt before checking his weapon and putting it back into the holster. "Lotta fuss over a guy who didn't belong in the desert."

"Foxglove was a local, or at least someone familiar with the territory. Can't imagine anyone could accidentally find that spring. Maybe he got drunk. People take too many pills, freeze to death, fall into rivers, wander into the wilderness, and die. That doesn't explain the wounds on his wrists or why his tent and handset were smashed. He didn't just go wandering from here after a bender. While I'm not ruling anything out, he wasn't at that watering hole by accident."

Walker shivered on the bunk at the back of the tent. "You gentlemen are worse than my old housemates. Bad enough I can't brush and floss my teeth. So how about letting me sleep?"

"How often did your 'housemates' tell you to shut up or get thumped?" Jodie said. When Walker didn't reply, he added, "That's what I thought." He picked up the lamp and exited the tent.

***

The advantage of an augmentation like Insight was a built-in alarm. It pinged inside Miles' head three times before he switched it off. The sensation made his teeth ache. The tingle lingered as he fought the fog in his head and got up. It surprised him he had slept for a few hours. Moving reminded him of fresh aches, no thanks to the saggy cot.

Faint light from the lamp outside allowed Miles to navigate the tent's interior.

Paxton Walker snored softly. The dog raised his head and whined.

"You coming or staying?"

The animal stretched first and joined him as he took the lamp and went outside.

Past the toilet, a circle of crates marked a spot that served as a cooking pit for a rusted stove. The lamp sat in the dirt. Marshal Jodie was nowhere in sight.

Miles scanned the darkness. A few of the neighbors on the terrace below had lights on, but the rows of shacks were silent. Milky lights glowed from the main street and the bar.

2 a.m.

Miles instinctively patted the butt of his burner before following the footpath up the terrace. A few tents down, someone was out front and cooking on a small gas flame. They eyed Miles warily as he approached.

"You see the marshal pass this way?" Miles asked.

The figure switched off the stove and retreated into their tent.

"Nice talking to you."

Beyond lay only night, with a few shelters forming a cul-de-sac of bare dirt at the end of the terrace. It appeared lifeless. He inspected a cargo truck that looked like it had gotten bogged down in mud either years or eons ago, as if the earth itself had half-consumed it, trapping it forever like a bug in tree sap. The plastic windows were intact, but enough of the exposed doors and roof were pockmarked with holes that the cab had become clotted with soil and weeds.

The dog sniffed about but shrank as a cool breeze kicked up. With it came flecks of icy rain.

"Let's get back," Miles said.

Walker remained bundled on his cot, having taken the blankets from Jodie's bed to add to his own. "Remind the innkeeper my gratuity hinges upon my not freezing my assets and dying before morning."

Miles placed the lamp on the floor and turned it up. Walker squinted.

"This meeting you had with your friend Foxglove. Who else knew about it?"

"Just me."

"You arranged for the meetup on your own?"

Walker was up on his elbow and blinked away sleep. "I used one of my fellow guests' messaging services since we weren't given access to phones. But it was a secure communique, our arrangements made in private."

"Don't make me ask again."

"I'm telling you the truth. Why the interrogation at this hour?"

"Because maybe your contact was killed by someone who was also after you. I'd like to know what we're dealing with in this camp."

"Poor service, uncomfortable beds, and a meal that is surely eating a hole in my stomach."

Miles turned off the lamp, went back outside, and scanned the night. Surely Jodie had left for some unspoken reason and hadn't fallen victim to an attack. Miles would have heard. He didn't want to share his misgivings with Walker that something was amiss. If Jodie didn't return within the hour, it meant they had a problem. Miles would monitor the prisoner and wait for now.

Chapter Nine

As the minutes turned into hours and the last of the camp's lights went out, Miles fought to ignore the phantoms lurking in the black.

The night was far from quiet. A trill erupted from some unknown bird or animal. It repeated a few times before growing still. A soft rustling nearby, the scrape of sand or pebbles disturbed, caused him to search for targets, but Insight yielded nothing and the noise didn't repeat. A high-pitched *peep* was followed by a flying shape that swooped past overhead.

A bat, Miles guessed. He resisted the urge to turn on the lamp and tried to keep himself concealed in case someone in camp was watching.

The familiar ache in his stomach grew. The unease of not knowing. The suspicion something horrible had happened to Marshal Jodie. No evidence to suggest anything had, and he tried to stifle his imagination. He'd have to search for him. But stumbling about with the prisoner would only result in more complications.

The sky took color. Ultramarine followed by cobalt, and the clouds of silver, then pink. What was the saying about red skies? He couldn't remember and didn't want to be distracted by reading anything Insight might know.

Paxton Walker emerged bundled in a bedroll.

"Stay inside," Miles said.

"My apologies, marshal, but what I have isn't waiting."

He almost stumbled over the dog as he went to the chem toilet. Miles pulled the dog closer and only partially turned away. Someone was coming, pedaling their way down the trail. Miles kept a hand on his pistol as the bicyclist zipped past without a word.

An engine started up somewhere down the slope. A quad bike with a trailer loaded with tools and bundled gear went puttering off across a lot and turned onto the main drag.

So there were vehicles, one at least.

Walker finished and struggled momentarily with his cuffed wrists to get his pants up. "Is Marshal Jodie securing our ride?"

"Never mind him. I want you back in the tent. I want you to stay there until we bring you out."

"Where is he?"

"Get inside now."

Walker vanished through the flap. "At the risk of being impudent," he said from inside the tent, "will there be tea before we set out? I find myself parched and a bit peckish."

"You and me both."

The shy neighbor was once again outside and cooking something in a frying pan. Smelled savory. There was enough light out to navigate easily. The cot inside the tent creaked. Walker was getting comfortable again. Miles couldn't wait any longer. He headed down the terrace towards the center of camp.

On the thoroughfare, two riders on horseback led two more horses burdened down with supplies. A herd of goats ambled past under the guide of a shepherd and a shaggy gray dog that paid Miles' own animal no mind.

Several people were walking towards the bar and heading inside. Jayakarta was with them. She was assisting an elderly man who walked with two canes in either hand. They were settling down at the same table as the night before. Jaya had them link hands and led them in a prayer. Tanni was behind the bar reading but paused to glare at Miles.

He waited at the door for the prayer to finish.

The group raised their heads, and one of them read aloud as the others listened.

Jaya noticed Miles. "You should join us, marshal. We pray Purity here and are open to all faiths. Plus, there's tea."

"I spent the last of my coin. Have you seen Marshal Jodie?"

"I haven't. You were staying up in the guest tents?"

"Yeah. He's probably around somewhere. Sorry to disturb you."

She caught up with him as he walked further along the street. There were others out, some washing up, others cooking, and more preparing tools and packs. No vehicles.

"You're concerned," she said. "When did you last see him?"

"He's probably checking up on something. Doesn't need me to baby-sit him."

"I understand why you'd be uneasy. Is this your first trip so far south?"

He glanced at her. "What makes you think that?"

"Facial expression. Body language. I have an instinct for that. Runs in the family. Most obvious is you appeared surprised that people here pay with coin instead of credits."

"I get it. If there's no network and you have folks scamming people, it makes sense to have a fallback system of exchange."

"It's different out here in more ways than that. Some feel Seraph has become everything it separated itself from. Taxation, stifling oversight, corruption."

"You're probably right. I was in River City not too long ago. Seraph's a new skin on an old beast, but that's part of what makes a civilization."

She smirked. "That's cynical."

"It is. But then it's up to us to do what we can to improve it. We don't give up."

"But you left River City."

"Family's in Seraph now," he said. "So I came out. What brings you out to the boonies?"

"Crippling debt. Plus, I fill a need here. I was a nurse in Seraph for a while. Manna needed a doctor and offered to cover my needs."

"This camp isn't that big. I'm guessing there's no mayor or government. The Alcott sisters?"

"They're what allows this place to function," she said. "They provide a stabilizing element, facilitate trade, offer protection."

"You're close enough to Seraph. The marshals and the Red District militia are supposed to take care of that."

"You're new here. I sense a sincerity to you. I hope you protect that quality. It's fragile."

"You'll have to excuse me. I need to get back to my prisoner."

The bartender's father was running in their direction. "Marshal? Ruthie Alcott wants to see you."

"Why?"

The man shook his head as if the question wasn't important. "Something about the other marshal. He's hurt."

Miles followed him across camp to a winding lane that led to an upper terrace. Wire fences marked off pens where livestock might have once been kept, but not now. One shack had a chicken coop with a few emaciated hens behind a screen of makeshift mesh tangled with weeds. They were pecking about in the dirt.

They approached a house comprised of several joined domes, an outdated hab design not common since the war. Each module was fabricated in a Meridian manufacturing plant and then flown to its desired location, a logistical difficulty since flight mostly remained off the table since the end of the war.

The place appeared freshly painted. Dried wreaths hung on the double doors. A pergola wrapped in honeysuckle ran along one side of the home. A potted vegetable garden appeared healthy, with peppers and lemons hanging heavy. Beyond were a shed and compost bins. Large, durable lounge chairs made of wood were set out in front. A tidy, comfortable desert abode for a furious pair of ogre sisters who might have summoned Miles to murder him. He resisted the urge to check the charge on his burner.

The barkeep knocked. "Ms. Alcott? I have the other marshal."

"Bring him in," a voice called.

Miles looked for the dog to get him under control, but he was off inspecting the garden. Miles went inside.

The entry dome was replete with potted ferns and other plants. A low circular table had a stack of paper ledgers and a ring of benches and seats all beneath a skylight. The air smelled earthy and humid. An open sliding door led to an interior atrium thick with palms and vegetation growing from stone-lined flower beds. From an archway leading to the next dome, Ruthie Alcott appeared, her red hair a wild tousle hanging over her face and down to her shoulders.

"Where's Marshal Jodie?" Miles asked.

Ruthie had a white towel in her hands and was wiping her fingers. "This way."

She led him through a larger dome separated by dividers but with an open ceiling. If Miles didn't know he was in Manna, he would have placed the eclectically furnished house someplace in Seraph, not in the same rarified neck of the woods as the Fishes, but in a nice neighborhood.

Miles strained his ears and kept his eyes moving. There was no sign of Dora.

Sheer curtains covered smaller doorways. Ruthie pushed a drape aside and ducked into a room.

Marshal Jodie lay on a plush bed beneath a mountain of sheets and blankets. His head was propped up on pillows. His eyes were closed, and he breathed through his open mouth, which was frothy with spittle. His shirt hung on a chair, and it appeared to have been cut to pieces.

"What happened?"

Ruthie placed the towel into a hamper. "Horace here found him out on Main Street unconscious. They got me and we brought him here. Thought at first he tied one on with a bottle of mescal, but then he didn't wake up."

She uncovered him. He still wore his underclothes. His body trembled, and his arms were curled to his chest. Miles got closer and felt Jodie's face. It was warm and sticky with sweat. At the side of his neck was a plum-colored bruise.

Ruthie said, "Guessed an allergic reaction to something, at least until I saw the mark."

Bug bite? Snake? Miles leaned in and let Insight scan the wound. Nothing on file that matched the symptoms, not that Insight kept extensive medical lore in storage. He needed access to Seraph net. Better yet, a doctor.

Miles checked Jodie's eyes. They stared blankly forward, the pupils dilated. His breathing had a rattle to it.

"Where's Jaya?" he asked. "She's Manna's closest thing to a doctor, isn't she?"

"I wanted you here first. I know where to find Jaya. She has her group in the bar."

"What's stopping you from bringing her?"

"Because I have my reservations involving her. I was hoping you knew something about Marshal Jodie that I don't. If this was just a seizure, and the mark on his body something else, then he could ride this out. You have a prisoner you're watching. Bring him here and we can see how Jodie does."

Miles took one of Jodie's hands. It remained clenched tight, resisting his efforts to pry it open. "Jaya's a nurse, isn't she? He's suffering. Why wouldn't you involve her?"

"Because strange things happen in Manna. The last thing I want is for a marshal to die."

"If she's a nurse, we could avoid that. What aren't you telling me about her?"

"Horace, wait outside."

Horace departed. The dog took his place, sniffing about before settling in near Miles' feet. The giant woman rounded the bed and wetted down a fresh cloth from a pitcher on a side table. She blotted the marshal's face.

"Manna rests at the border of two worlds, marshal. Marshal Jodie has been around long enough to understand things don't work the same here as they do in Seraph. Further to the south, where your patrols never go, are places where laws are what each settlement decides upon, or there're none at all. We're self-sufficient out of necessity. We abide by enough of Seraph decree to receive help with the worst of the worst. That's the role you marshals play. But more often than not, we need to deal with our own as best as we can. That's my job. Manna hangs on by a thread. Some residents here could never function in Seraph."

"So they make it here and get by. What does this have to do with Jaya?"

"We need all the help we can get. You think a proper doctor or a good nurse could function in these conditions and live like we do?"

Miles searched the unease on her face. "Doctors and nurses are just people. There's been greater hardships than what I see in this camp. You're saying you need her here."

"Desperately."

"So, is she not a real nurse?"

"She's real, and a good one," Ruthie said. "Talented. Brilliant, maybe. Probably could have had what you'd call a good career back in Seraph or elsewhere. But she's here now with us. I don't want anyone, especially you, doing anything to scare her off."

"So she has something in her past. And right now, I don't care. If she had a role with what happened to Marshal Jodie, you really want that kind of person in your camp?"

"I don't think she would hurt a fly and I don't believe she had anything to do with what happened to the marshal. I'm saying I don't want her spending any more time with *you*. She might let something slip, and I don't know you enough to know what you'll do."

"I'm not here for her. We have no warrant for her—"

Ruthie raised a meaty hand. "Let me finish. She's not in your system, at least not under this face and this name. I looked. What I'm more concerned about is that one of you marshals will do or say something or ask questions like you lawmen do that will send her running. She's fragile. Whatever happened in her past hasn't caught up with her, and I'm going to delay that as long as possible."

Miles nodded, hoping that he understood. "Marshal Jodie needs her help. If that means we don't fill out a report on what happened and why, that's easy enough. Her name stays out of it. Jaya's not the only one with a past. Am I reading you right?"

"And what about that fancy eye and brain of yours?"

"Not so fancy. She didn't ring any bells when I saw her, and out here, there's no way for me to search. I want her here to get the marshal well. Think about how much worse it will be for Manna if he dies."

Ruthie clenched her jaw, perhaps contemplating breaking Miles in half and burying her marshal problem out back inside her compost bin. "I'll have Horace fetch her."

Chapter Ten

"Why didn't you get me sooner?"

Miles didn't have an answer for Jaya as she examined Marshal Jodie. His shivering hadn't subsided. Appeared worse, if Miles were to judge. While his body continued to sweat, he felt chilled and his jaw chattered.

Jaya only had a tablet computer to run her diagnosis. Without a network, it would only have access to whatever files she had downloaded. She rummaged through a neatly arranged soft zip case of medical supplies. Pills in wrappers were in one pouch, alongside an injector and a small suite of surgical tools. She produced an infrared thermometer and took Jodie's temperature before manually checking his pulse.

"Well?" Ruthie Alcott prompted.

"Stable. He's breathing. He'll continue to breathe. I know nothing about him to try any medicine, and without knowing what's in his system, it would be a crap shoot."

"You can't pray him better."

"I know that," Jaya snapped. "He needs a hospital. At the very least, we should get him hooked up to an autodoc. We don't have one here. It means someone has to take him to Seraph. I understand none of you have a vehicle."

"My tool pusher hasn't brought ours back yet. Best we can do is a horse or quad bike, and it's too far a ride to make that work, I'm guessing."

"It would be a risk. Better off leaving him in bed where I can observe him. I can get him hydrated; we have supplies for that. I'll intervene if he takes a turn. Otherwise, it's watch and wait."

Miles asked Ruthie, "Does your tool pusher usually take this long checking on an antenna?"

"Not if he doesn't want to get thumped. That said, it's a ways out, a rough ride, and he might have taken a detour while he had my runner." When Miles waited for more, she sighed and shook her head. "There's a couple of places with whores who don't want to live by our rules. Also a watering hole where they serve hootch that can strip the grease off an engine block."

"Be good to know where he is and when he's coming back."

"It's a few kilometers southeast up on the Chalk Crest. If he's not back by noon, I'll send Horace out hunting."

"I have a prisoner I need to check on. Thank you both for caring for Jodie."

Rain pattered down in heavy irregular drops, leaving dimples in the gray dust on the trails between the homes. The air felt muggy and carried a weight to it, and the brooding clouds promised more. But for now, the rain was more of a nuisance.

The dog kept to the trail ahead of Miles as he returned to the tent.

Paxton Walker was gone.

Miles made a cursory search, but the blankets were empty. Outside, the dog had run off to the nearby tent with the shy neighbor. He was sniffing about the stove and entry flap and barked. As Miles hurried to collect the animal, he heard Walker inside.

"Why, my dear madam, you don't require a fancy stage, a sound system, or even proper lighting. Theater is wherever a play is presented, needing nothing more than a single actor with the words on their lips spoken in an authentic voice. Everything else is window dressing. Of course, air conditioning is nice, as is an ample backroom to collect one's thoughts. But truly, there should be nothing stopping your fine suburb in staging a production of your choosing, if you're footing the bill."

Miles pulled back the flap, expecting to see Walker and the shy neighbor. Instead, he found his fugitive and Dora Alcott. Walker sat on a three-legged stool, his cuffed hands gripping a metal cup. Dora rested on the floor of the tent, legs crisscrossed, with several pieces of meager furniture shoved out of the way against the back wall. Her shotgun lay on her lap. She grasped a jug in one oversized hand and eyed Miles blearily.

Walker raised his cup in a salute. His cheeks were a brighter pink than usual. "Why marshal, there you are."

Miles placed a hand on his shoulder. "Why aren't you where I told you to be?"

"I was entertaining one of Manna's community leaders and informing her of my services."

"You don't have services." He took Walker by the arm. "Dora, you'll excuse me while I take my prisoner back where he belongs."

Dora thrust the jug in Miles' direction. "Drink."

"I don't partake. I don't react well to alcohol."

"Drink," she repeated with a throaty growl.

"It's still early and I haven't even had breakfast."

Her face fixed into a snarl. She began to get up, but paused when Miles accepted the jug. He took a whiff and caught the astringent vapors of something potent. "If I take a sip, can we leave?"

Dora had murder in her eyes. Miles knew this wasn't the time to shoot his way out of a problem. Hadn't had a drink since the war. Seeing no other options, he tilted the jug back and let his lips get wet. They instantly tingled. Miles tried to hand the jug back.

She pushed it towards him, her voice low and firm. "Sit, take a drink, or there'll be two marshals who need the nurse."

He sat. Braced himself. Took a swig. It was worse than he imagined, the burn instant, the taste like rubbing alcohol, the vapors singeing his nostrils as flame went down his esophagus. Heat clawed up his face. He belched and forced himself to keep it down.

"See?" Walker said. "Told you this was the better of the two law enforcement agents calling on your charming hamlet."

The dog did a quick check of the tent and inserted his nose into Dora's armpit. She absentmindedly stroked the animal's spine. "No more talk from you, Paxton. Time for me and the Metal Head to speak."

Miles took a deep, cooling breath and handed the jug back to her. "I'm not a Metal Head."

"Metal Head. Marshal. Neither are welcome here. Only difference? I get to shoot Metal Heads."

"Now that we have that cleared up, Marshal Jodie is hurt. Walker here is my prisoner. I need to get both back to Seraph. To do that, I have to find a ride. I'm taking him to your sister's, where we'll wait if Marshal Jodie recovers."

As he spoke, Dora took a swallow before thrusting the jug once again into Miles' hands. "Drink!"

"I'm not going to do anyone any good if I get loaded. And your sister is going to be mad with all of us."

"My sister is always mad. Needs to control her temper. You found a dead man at the High Spring."

"We did."

Dora nodded and lowered her gaze. The dog licked her. She was rubbing his ears. "Man you call Foxglove stayed with me whenever he came to Manna. His name is Eddie. Ruthie never liked Eddie, but she doesn't tell me who I sleep with."

Miles took a polite sip. "Did your sister dislike him enough to hurt him?"

"Ruthie isn't dumb like me. She wouldn't kill him. Dead people bring the marshals. And I was with my sister the last few days."

"Is there anyone else here that would hurt Eddie?"

"I wouldn't let that happen." She snatched the jug away and chugged before setting the container aside. She sniffed and wiped her nose and eyes. "How did he die?"

"We don't know. We didn't have time for a proper investigation. He had a tent set up, but the spring isn't that far from here."

"He did his business wherever it took him. But he would come back. He won't come back anymore. You need a car."

"Ruthie says yours is with your tool pusher checking on the antenna. She's offered to help."

Dora waved the comment away like it was a bug. "My sister will do what's good for the camp. Doubt she told you about what happened to Jodie."

"What do you think happened?"

"He had a dart in him. Did Ruthie show you that?"

"He had an injury, maybe a sting from an insect."

"No, not a sting. Hit with a weapon."

He tried to push the dazed sensation from his brain. "By who? Did Ruthie attack him, or one of her men?"

"No. That wouldn't be good for the camp. I'll tell you more, but I want to know if the same thing happened to Eddie."

"That will take time. Right now, I have my hands full. We can investigate what happened to Eddie when we come back."

"You might not make it back. Ruthie won't hurt a marshal. People in Manna wouldn't, either. But there are others. Bad people."

"That are here?"

"If you're smart, you'll go. Maybe Marshal Jodie will be left alone, since Ruthie is protecting him."

"I have my prisoner. I won't just leave."

"Then find out what happened to my Eddie. If you do, I'll get you your ride. Then you can take Paxton, take Jodie, and never come back to Manna again."

Chapter Eleven

"You heard her," Paxton Walker said. "We need to get out of here. If someone's gunning for marshals, you're not safe. And if someone attacked Foxglove—Eddie—then maybe they're after me too."

He waited for Miles to reply. They were outside on the terrace, the sun cresting over the lip of the canyon to the west. Dora was still inside the tent, making baby talk to Miles' dog.

Miles rubbed his forehead with his fist, trying to drive away the light-headedness. "What were you and Eddie into that would have people willing to kill?"

"It's like I told you."

"Tell me again."

"He was going to be my ride to New Pacific."

"What made you pick him?"

"I was desperate and he was available. He has—had—a reputation to get anyone or anything where they needed to go. Reliable service, dear marshal, is a rarity in these troubled times."

If you're smart, you'll go.

Dora's words gnawed at him. While her forthrightness could be a front, her candor felt genuine. Miles wanted to kick himself for not being more thorough with the dead man at the spring. Then it would be a matter of reviewing what he saw, using Insight to check over the images. The man had been bound. But there had been no obvious sign of being shot by a tranquilizer dart, or stung, except for the fact that if he had been paralyzed like Marshal Jodie, it would explain his death.

Walker was sweating. "We're leaving then, right? You get me back to my penitentiary. I'll face whatever markup to my sentence for my misdeeds during my escape."

"What about your feet? Don't think you'll make it far."

"I will overcome, sir marshal. We procure water and provisions and rely on the universe to bring us a blessing in the form of a mount or a ride or a functioning signal so you can summon aid."

"Why are you so nervous? Is there a reason you think anyone besides us is after you?"

A titter escaped Walker's lips. "A man hears things. Even in River City, there's hearsay about the wastes to the south, and other places never blessed by the unity spread by Meridian. Some rumors have the mark of truth. Even your own office has its own that go missing, and rarely in places within city limits. But it's not just lawmen. Tax officials. Surveyors. Even academics trying to link the age of man on Earth with our current epoch, and ones wanting to study the culture of those who survived in between."

"Outlaws. They're nothing new."

Walker shook his head. "What kind of outlaw leaves coins on their victim?"

Miles thought about the money he had found. Criminals were stupid, careless, and often in a hurry. What other reason might there be to not bother with coins? If Foxglove had been murdered, Miles doubted the killers had been squeamish. But if Dora was offering them a runner, then a trip back to the spring might be the best way to secure a ride.

Head off on foot with Walker? Hole up at Ruthie's and wait for Marshal Jodie to recover? Neither was a sound option if there really was someone gunning for them. The silence in the camp had reasserted itself but for someone hammering away at something on the next terrace down. The break-of-dawn rush was over.

Miles felt a prickling on his neck. Nerves, or was someone watching him?

Both, probably.

No choice was worse than a poor one.

"You're going to wait here," Miles said.

"What?"

"Dora's going to look after you. You, in turn, are going to watch my dog. I'm going to check out the spring and be back hopefully by late afternoon."

"You can't...you can't..."

"I can, and that's what I'm going to do. You're the prisoner here. And if you slip away, know that I'll catch up with you, and you'll wish whatever bad guy took care of your pal Foxglove got to you first."

***

Miles could only hope his warning to Walker came across with its intended gravitas rather than a poor impression of a serial cop spouting cliches. Dora had been agreeable enough, and she brightened when Miles also asked her to look after the dog.

Whether Eddie was Dora's lover, friend, or a convenient lay, she had been crying. Miles felt the familiar crush inside the center of his chest, wanting to comfort but knowing doing his job was the only thing that might bring closure. Until they got a signal out, no help would be coming.

What about leaving Jodie in Ruthie's hands? Perhaps she was, as her sister said, interested in the camp's wellbeing. An executed marshal *would* mean trouble. If she wanted them dead, she could have killed Marshal Jodie and likewise have attacked him.

Too many other questions lingered. Why shoot Jodie with a tranq gun in the first place? Had his assailants been interrupted or scared away? And was it Ruthie who had actually found him?

Other unmet denizens of Manna might have differing opinions on what was good for the camp.

He began walking, heading to the thoroughfare, and starting the hike back towards what Dora had called the High Spring. The more he thought about it, he knew being alone would be a risk. Yet he liked the idea that he might learn what had happened to Foxglove, especially if it could illuminate what else was going on in Manna. It would also give him the opportunity to eyeball the malfunctioning antenna where Ruthie had sent her repair person.

Southeast up on the Chalk Crest, Ruthie had said. A rough ride.

He wished he had asked for directions.

He paused by the town sign, listening and scanning.

A horse and rider were cantering towards him from camp. Jaya was wrapped in layers, wearing goggles and a cap with flaps on the back and sides. The horse was a spotted pony with brown rear flanks. Its nostrils flared as Jaya drew up next to Miles.

"You were going to walk?" she asked.

"Manna has a specific lack of cars."

"That would take you half a day, assuming you know where it is." She offered him a hand. "Climb on." She helped him up into the saddle.

"What about Marshal Jodie?"

"I summoned one of my students to monitor him."

"So how'd you hear where I'm going?"

"I didn't, but it's a reasonable guess. I saw you leaving town without your prisoner. With no hospital, I know there's not much more I could do for Marshal Jodie. I was on my way to ride to the antenna myself so I could contact the nearest camps for help."

"That would be good. But I'm not going there yet. Dora wants me to check on something. You know how to get to the High Spring?"

Chapter Twelve

"High Spring and the camp's antenna are in the opposite direction," Jaya said. "Just so you know."

She rode the horse down the soft sand of what might have once been a streambed at the center of the canyon. The ridges rose higher than Miles remembered, and the pass they were entering looked unfamiliar. The gray rock formations blended with one another. According to Insight, the direction was right, but he felt turned around.

Her tongue clicked. She gave the pony a gentle nudge before it would climb a crumbling bank. Once up the slope, it kept to its amble, and Jaya did nothing to quicken the pace.

She took a stim stick out of a pocket and was soon exhaling a plume of vapor that reeked of peppermint. "Oh lord, I needed that. Can't do it in camp."

Miles was failing at getting comfortable, with the rear of the saddle digging into his butt. "Seems like anything goes in Manna. What's stopping you?"

"Some in my Purity circle are quite devout. No drink, no stims. Wouldn't want to set a stumbling block before them."

"I thought Purity was each to their own, but together."

She took another drag and held it in for a moment before exhaling. "Welcome to small town life. Prayer circle in a bar, but none of my students will taste a drop of Horace's finest. Do we call it irony? Manna. A blessing taken for granted. Areca, tobacco, agave, fermentations—all gifts from our creator. But some in their path of faith would abstain and insist others do, too.”

“Teach them about the power of moderation.”

“Maybe one day.” She offered him the stim stick.

“No, thanks. I appreciate you taking the detour. This would have been tricky without the horse and you along as a guide.”

She waved the stim stick. “Here to serve.”

“Ruthie tells me I need to tip-toe around you. That if I do or say the wrong thing, you’re going to run.”

“She’s possessive. Like my Purity students, she doesn’t want me to slip through her fingers.”

Miles clung ever tighter to her as they traversed another rolling section of ground. “Nice to be wanted.”

Jaya made a non-committal sound. “It’s funny. At first, I thought *you* were the senior marshal. Serves me right for making judgment. Without a map or the net, you can get lost. Takes a while to understand the places down here. Manna isn’t its full name, you know.”

“What is it, then?”

“Where We Waited for the Manna. One of the old timers used to remake the full sign until she died. Ruthie thought an image makeover would attract a better class of resident. Like me, for instance. But the old name? Tells a story, doesn’t it?”

“The name could be taken two ways,” Miles said. “There a big grave-yard from a mass starvation here I haven’t seen yet?”

“These hills and rocks are full of old bones. Can’t say what happened to the camp founders. Before the return, like so many places with the strange names. Must have survived for a while. They either moved on or they didn’t. An object lesson, to be certain. Don’t wait for someone or something to drop a blessing in your lap when it’s in your power to go out and get it for yourself.”

“Another topic for your circle.”

They were at a hard packed but narrow track that wound up an em-bankment. Miles thought they’d have to dismount, but after Jaya clicked her tongue, the horse clambered up it with only a few stomach-churning moments where Miles had to hang on for dear life to avoid falling.

"You had a dog with you," Jaya prompted.

"Left him with my prisoner, and they're both with Dora."

"Placing a lot of trust in the Alcott sisters."

"They're what serves as a local government."

She laughed. "Is that what you call them? Ruthie'd get a kick out of that. As small as Manna is, plenty of folks would beg to differ. Ruthie just banks on the fact that most people are lazy and don't want to fuss with being in charge when they're busy scraping by. Plus, she has Dora."

"You seem to get along fine with them."

"Nah. I'm just as lazy as the next person. I don't confuse the Alcott's reign as legitimate governance. They're thugs. You might do well to remember that."

"From what I've gathered over my years, it's not so much different in Meridian or Seraph. Just more paperwork."

They were climbing switchbacks. Again, not the route along which they had descended, but he recognized the rock formations. Based on the distance and direction traveled, Insight confirmed the spring lay ahead. They had just completed a more direct route and came out on top of a crown of stones, with the spring below and the skeletal fingers of dead trees on the crest in plain view.

The rockpile grave lay in shadows.

"Not an easy place to find," Jaya said.

"Our jailbird led us here. Best if you wait with the horse."

They both dismounted. Jaya found a patch of withered grass for the horse to graze while Miles went to the grave and began unstacking rocks.

Jaya appeared next to him a moment later and crouched to help. "If I'm the responsible party for the town's physical health, I should know if we're facing down a pest. Besides, a dead body should be properly handled."

"With one horse, we're not getting it off this ridge today."

She pushed aside a few stones, revealing Eddie's feet. Miles placed the last of the rocks next to him and brushed dirt away from the body. A rank aroma made him gag. He took a moment before leaning close. Checked Eddie's neck and face and arms. Even clotted with dust, the wrist wounds were obvious. The swelling had only worsened, with purple discoloration setting in.

Jaya pushed the shirt away. "Hardly ideal circumstances for a necropsy. Look here."

Low on Eddie's left flank above the hip was a small brown circle. She took a first aid kit from a fanny pack and produced a pair of scissors. They made quick work of the undershirt's fabric. A round wound on the skin mirrored the swollen lump on Marshal Jodie's neck.

She pointed at one wrist. "Hit with whatever stung him, tied up, and then what?"

"Found him at the side of the spring. No sign of any cords or zip ties."

"Like they were planning on coming back for him?"

"I don't think so," he said. "Looks like he might have dragged himself up here."

"While paralyzed. That sounds like a horrible way to go, inching along while the sun bakes you alive. How far did he crawl?"

Miles stood and brushed off his knees. Realized he had been holding his breath against the stench and sucked in air. He stared out at the spring and the rocks above. "Maybe he didn't crawl."

The climb to the top of the spring reminded him of the scramble up to the lookout with Santabutra. Only from here there was no command-ing view of Seraph, just more rocks and desert.

Lengths of frayed hemp rope still dangled from the thickest branches of the dead tree. Somehow, Eddie had slipped out of them, only to plummet to the ground below next to the spring. Just high enough to be a fatal fall. No accident. But what Miles found next sent a jolt of ice down his spine.

A piece of wood was nailed to the top of the tree. Someone had scratched a single word in charcoal.

GUILTY.

Chapter Thirteen

"Rules out a bug bite." Jaya had clambered up behind him, standing upright on the top of the rocks, appearing unafraid of the lethal drop to either side of the ridge.

Miles scanned the rocks around the tree, keeping crouched with a hand on the trunk. "Rules out a robbery, too."

"Unless someone got creative and wanted to throw off the scent of anyone coming to investigate."

"Pretty elaborate, dragging a man all the way up here. From my experience, unless the perp is stoned, they want to get away from a dead body. Any way to know if he was alive when he was strung up?"

"I'm a nurse, not a forensic tech. Give me a lab and an AR suite? Maybe I can tell you a story. But this? This is pure psycho."

Miles discovered scuff marks on the rocks from hard-soled shoes. "Ninety kilos of an uncooperative, unconscious, or dead person. Not a one-man job."

"Not just bad men out here. How about genetically modified women?"

"This look like something the Alcotts might have done?"

Jaya made a face. "They're ball busters. This seems elaborate, even for Ruthie. And why 'guilty'?"

"Seems remote for a sign to warn others. Whatever Eddie did, what happened to him feels personal."

"Remote, but not completely out of sight. While he was on the tree, anyone coming to the High Spring would see him. Either they didn't tie him well, or he had enough strength at the end to wiggle out of the ropes."

The location where they had found the body was a likely landing spot. Freeing himself had been his last act.

Miles wasn't normally afraid of heights, but he closed his eyes for a moment to let his stomach settle. "Let's get down from here."

On his descent, Miles surveyed the horizon. One hilltop had the Manna antenna planted on it, but he couldn't locate it. He returned to Eddie's side, committing what he could to memory and his Insight module before placing rocks back over him.

Jaya was in the shade by the spring, drinking water from her hands before splashing some over her face. With the clouds came humidity, and by the time Miles had covered the body, he was damp with sweat. The smell of the man clung to his nose like a heat rash. He joined Jaya for a drink. The water was cool, instant relief for his parched throat. A sandy mineral flavor didn't deter him from drinking more until he satisfied his thirst.

She was watching him with interest. "So it's confirmed something nasty happened here. Maybe you knew that, and this just underscores what you've learned. Without communication and with your partner disabled, you could go for help. You could take my horse. I'd make it back to camp well enough."

"Can't risk it. Whoever did this targeted Jodie. If there's a chance I can send a message and summon help before nightfall, that's what I'm going to do."

"What if you have to choose?"

"What? Between Jodie and my prisoner?"

"There's also your own neck to think about. Whoever did this to Eddie and Jodie isn't afraid of a badge or a burner. You leave now, you get to one of the northern camps sometime tomorrow. Get your help. I'll make sure Jodie stays safe."

Miles stood and wiped his damp palms on his trousers. "If the perp targeted Jodie, he might be out there willing to take a run at me. They found Eddie all the way up here. That's someone with a grudge. If that includes marshals, I won't abandon Jodie."

She chuckled humorlessly. "Doesn't matter how far you run, I guess. If someone wants you bad enough, they'll catch up with you. Is that the case with you, marshal?"

"What makes you think I'm running from something?"

"It's the desert. Everyone's running from someone. Or something. So what's your demon?"

"Getting stuck out in the rain. You know where the camp's antenna is?"

They rode down the same steep track, the horse going faster than Miles would have preferred, with Jaya seeming to allow the animal to set its own pace. He was grateful when they got to the soft sand at the bottom of the canyon. It didn't take long before they were once again riding between configurations of rock that they hadn't passed before, with striations in shades of gray and blue marking ages of earth and water predating anyone ever having lived in the region.

He kept his eyes open for any signs of movement. With the details of Eddie's death laid bare, the dangers of the southern region were no longer an abstraction. A robbery, revenge, or an escalated encounter with another criminal were understandable motives Miles could get his head around. But now he had confirmation that monsters lurked in the ravines and wastes, a familiar flavor of the worst evils he had faced in River City yet distinct in its otherness, as so much else he was growing accustomed to since coming to Seraph.

They were heading towards a broad plain where the walls fell away to flat, exposed stone and hardpan. Was this the same stretch of ground across which they had followed Paxton Walker? Perhaps close. But here were clumps of reddish-brown rocks, with sickly scrub and thistles growing everywhere.

"I thought the antenna would be at the top of one of the hills," he said.

"It is. Didn't Ruthie tell you? There's more than one. We have a big antenna on the heights, but there are a couple of smaller receivers out here."

Solar panels lay ahead of them, a ring of energy collectors arrayed around a cluster of dwarf towers. The communication signal equipment had a jury-rigged quality, with different color grids of steel held in place by tension cables of various sizes. A windsock flapped with the breeze, and a wind speed meter spun at the top of a sensor spire. On a plastic rod fixed with twisted low-gauge wire, a yellow triangle flag of cloth likewise shifted in the moving air.

"Who owns this place?" Miles asked.

"My understanding is it's a co-op. Alcotts and a few people from the nearest camps work out who pays for what and who fixes things when they break. An ad hoc arrangement, to be sure."

"I don't suppose you have a map on your device you could share? Be good to know where the other camps are."

"You really are unprepared."

She brought the horse to a stop and slid down from the saddle. The animal started turning when Miles tried to do the same. He got out of the saddle, lowered himself, and jumped aside to avoid getting a foot trampled.

"Didn't train you in riding in the service?" Jaya asked.

"How'd you know I was in the service?"

"Thought all you old timer marshals were."

Miles had his device out. No signal. He looked at the antenna array and walked around it. A battery box stood open, the battery missing. A conduit to the solar panels lay severed in the dirt. He found a breaker box and flipped it up and down, but the indicator light remained dark.

"Battery's gone," Miles said. "And see this conduit? Someone took this station offline. This happen often?"

"You'd need to ask Ruthie or someone who's been in town longer. Nothing like this has happened since I've been here. Thief or vandal, I'd guess. So stupid. Outsiders pass through from time to time, even Red Banner militia. Some don't understand how important a com relay like this is to everyone living nearby."

"Heavy battery. Probably not stolen by someone on horseback."

A blanket with angular geometric patterns was laid out beneath the yellow flag. On it were earthenware dishes with lids, jugs, bowls of red, green, and orange peppers, prickly pears, and some metal odds and ends. A second blanket lay next to it.

He picked up a prickly pear. Soft and ripe. "Trading post?"

"Yeah. Some people out here are hermits, or don't want visitors. So they use the springs or, in this case, the relay station, as a market on the honor system. Trade or coin goes on the other blanket."

"There's no one around. That mean they're watching?"

"Probably."

If there were traders in the desert, they weren't close enough to see. He put the fruit back in the bowl. A thief had stolen the signal station's battery, while a hermit scrapper had laid out his wares for anyone to take, relying on mutual trust to receive fair payment.

And what was the desert communities' penalty for petty theft? What crime had Eddie committed to result in his guilty verdict and death sentence?

Miles found tire tracks. Bike, motorcycle, but nothing as large as a runner. Dried horse droppings lay in a pile. Had the battery thief taken the battery with them, or was it possible they had hidden it so it could be reinstalled? Miles didn't want to spend more time out in the desert than necessary. He needed to get back to Walker and Marshal Jodie.

"Any of the hermits use drone delivery?" he asked. "Delivery dogs or otherwise?"

"It's possible. Not enough charge stations, at least as far as I've seen. What are you thinking?"

"In case I need to send for backup. You say there's other towers we can check? Be good to know if we're dealing with a battery thief, or something else entirely."

Chapter Fourteen

The man riding towards them sat hunched on a milky white buckskin with a swayed back and charcoal mane. A blanket served as the horse's saddle. The rider wore a tall backpack tied down with twine. His peaked hat brim didn't conceal his angled jawline and sharp nose.

He had his hand up in a greeting as Miles and Jaya rode towards him across the loose earth in the ravine's shade. They had been riding for an hour, her pony flagging. Supposedly, there was another antenna they could make at the top of a nearby crest. An easy ride, Jaya said, and one they could make before the day grew too late. It was the closest relay to Manna, and likely the one Ruthie had sent her tool pusher to check on first.

The rider brought his horse about, finally dropping his hand. "What news from the road?"

"Storm's coming," Jaya said.

"Aye, that it is. You're the Manna doctor. And that fellow with you?"

"I'm Marshal Kim."

The man raised his head as if to appraise Miles. Too far to get a clear view of his face. "A Seraph marshal. Heard one was passing through. Appears there's two of them now. Expecting trouble?"

"Routine patrol. What's your name, friend?"

"Doesn't look like routine, you sharing a saddle with the Manna doctor."

"Checking on the radio receivers. Someone made off with the battery of one. It's left everyone without communications. You probably noticed on your device."

"Don't carry one."

"There might be people in your camp who do. Have you seen anyone—"

"Don't stay with any of the camps," the man interrupted. "Least not one a marshal would choice to visit. As the Manna doctor might have told you, we take care of ourselves out here."

"I'm sure you do. But Seraph jurisdiction covers this area—"

"Seraph jurisdiction? You see paved roads and high rises and robot trucks and people in suits out here? You expect us to wait patiently like good pups who believe our betters in the city will descend their towers to show us ruth and charity?"

Miles hesitated before answering. Had handled his share of cranky people looking to get into an argument. "The folks in Manna are remarkably resilient. Everyone out here has to be. You don't need me to tell you that. But there's a broken piece of equipment some people rely on. If you hear or see anything, I'd appreciate it if you send word to Manna. Have a safe journey."

"That was...diplomatic," Jaya said after they had ridden on. The man was behind them and out of sight.

"Amazing what you can accomplish when you don't come out guns blazing."

"You never know out here. Plenty of thieves or people who might jump on a target of opportunity."

"My winning smile wins them over."

"Tower's up this way."

A winding trail up a hill led to a rocky knoll, where a single metal tower fixed with a dozen signal dishes stood among several boulders. A quad bike sat nearby.

"That's Ruthie's," Jaya said as she directed the horse to the base of the tower. "Her tool pusher is Ivan."

"Ivan?" Miles called. No answer. The wind picked up enough that

Miles would have lost his hat if he didn't plant his hand down on it. "He can't have gone far without his bike."

Someone sat at the base of the tower. As they got closer, Miles zoomed in. "Stay here."

He slid down from the saddle and approached.

Ivan the tool pusher was leaning forward, a cord around his neck. His skin was blue, his eyes bulging, and his dangling tongue told Miles the man was dead even as he checked for a pulse. Like Eddie at High Spring, his hands were tied tight behind him. The cord around his neck had no slack, placing the man in a difficult position to maintain to avoid strangulation.

Miles felt acid rising in his throat when he spotted a scrawled rectangle of plastic placed on Eddie's chest.

GUILTY.

"Is he...?" Jaya asked.

"Gone."

He rose and checked his device. Still nothing. The tower and its components appeared intact until Miles found a dangling section of severed wire linking the transmitter to a solar panel and power cell. A cursory inspection of the dead man's overalls found nothing except for a stim stick and a pack of condoms.

Miles stood up over the body. "This is bad. Eddie was up to something with his meeting at High Spring. But this? What do you know about Ivan?"

"Kept to himself. English wasn't good; spoke Russian and Mandarin. I don't think Ivan was his real name, but after being in Manna for even a short time, I'm guessing the same could be said for anyone."

He resisted the urge to ask about Jaya's name. Time for that later. A tool chest on the back of the runner stood open, with tools inside which, while a few were tarnished or rusty, were serviceable and no doubt worth something to a desert dweller. And the runner still had its key card in the ignition. Miles tried the engine. It didn't start. All the leads running between the power plant and the dash had been cut.

Jaya took a couple of deep breaths before making her own examination of the dead man. "Is the quad bike intact?

"Whoever did this messed it up. A few hours with the right parts, I could fix it."

"You ever see anything like this?"

"Nothing this deliberate. I don't know how Eddie and Ivan are connected, but someone had it out for them and knew where to find them."

"Remote places. Gave them time to do...this to them."

"I'm new to Seraph and newer to the desert here. Any rumors of anyone dispensing their own brand of frontier justice?"

She took out her stim stick and puffed on it. "Rumors? Sure. But nothing recent. I heard stories of people catching up with a pair of thieves who robbed a miner camp. Shot them down and left them to rot as a warning to the rest of their gang. But the name of the camp and the gang and the number of thieves change, depending on who you ask."

"Doesn't mean it didn't happen."

"Usually means it happened a long time ago."

Miles took a long look at the dead man. "Can't do anything for him now, not while I have a living prisoner who might be a target back in Manna."

Jaya brought the horse around and climbed on, steadying the mount before helping Miles up. Once again, abandoning a crime scene. But it couldn't be helped, and lingering to search for clues placed Walker at risk.

The sharp thundercrack and the impact landed simultaneously. The horse jerked and fell, rolling over and sending Miles and Jaya tumbling. Miles crawled away as the dying animal thrashed. The echo of the gunshot reverberated around them.

"Get to the rocks!" he shouted. As he moved towards cover, a second report washed over him. A stone near his head shattered, sending a spray of stinging debris across his face. He recoiled, changing direction, and pressing against the fallen horse. It was breathing hard, its lungs working like bellows. It cut loose with a miserable whine as it gnashed at the air. But it faded quickly, its body convulsing as its strength ebbed.

Miles tried to take in what he could of the higher ground around the hill, but he didn't dare raise his head. They were exposed to several superior vantage points. He could only hope the horse would shield him from the sniper. If the shooter changed position, they'd be dead.

"Jaya, you okay?"

"I'm alive. I'm behind a boulder."

"Stay there. I don't dare move. Keep your head down."

"Yeah."

The horse was taking its final breaths, each inhalation shallower than the last, until finally it shuddered and lay still. Miles strained his ears. The hilltop was silent. He tried to get a clear picture of the surrounding land-scape with his Insight module, but his mind was racing and his heart was hammering and he couldn't concentrate. He'd need to raise his head, and someone wouldn't need to be a good shot to hit him with a scoped rifle. And if his theory held up, there was more than one person out there.

Chapter Fifteen

"Law man?"

A shrill male voice called from somewhere below their hill. The horse's body remained uncomfortably warm as Miles continued to take cover pressed against it.

"Know you're up here, law man. You too, doc. You show your hands, you hear? Show your hands if you want any chance of walking out of here alive."

"Stay down," he hissed in Jaya's direction.

He had his hat off and peered up along the back of the saddle. Jaya remained behind the rocks, hugging her legs and keeping her head against her knees. He pulled his burner and set Insight to scanning, but he couldn't see anything.

"Don't want nothing to happen to you that isn't deserved, law man. But if you don't come out, it will go poorly for you, yes indeed."

The person shouting was louder now, perhaps just on the opposite side of the outcropping near the quad bike. If the man calling was alone, it would be the perfect time for Miles to make a break for Jaya and the superior cover. But the sniper might be watching, and he didn't dare raise his head another centimeter.

"Oh, ho-ho-ho, law man. Spotter says you got your light gun out. Drop it. Drop it now, or you'll learn what a mistake it is to bring that toy into the desert."

Miles raised the pistol, letting it dangle by the grip with its barrel down. He stood, his legs tingling from having been squeezed into the same position for so long. He set the burner down on the horse's flank.

"I'm here. My hands are up."

The man who came around the rocks had a black pistol raised in his hands. Perhaps thirty years old, he sported light chin hair and wore a brown peacoat and a hat with grass sticking in it at all angles. "You certainly surprised us, showing up here. Thought you were in Manna. We weren't expecting you to come up that trail where you did."

"I'm full of surprises. I'm Marshal Kim. What's your name, son?"

The man licked his lips and shifted his pistol to his left hand and back to his right. "There'll be time for introductions later. Later, when Gabriel comes, after he hears we caught you. Yes sir, we did."

He walked further around the rocks and got closer, his attention fully on Miles. Did he not see Jaya? Miles approached him slowly, keeping his hands up and his eyes on the man and his weapon. If he got close enough, her hiding place would remain out of his line of sight.

"That's far enough. Get on your knees."

Miles kept his voice low and slow. "Saw what you did to Ivan over there. And Eddie up at High Spring. Want to tell me what this is all about?"

The man shifted his gun between his hands again. His tongue kept creeping out of his mouth to moisten cracked lips. "What it's all about? What it's all about? If you knew, if you only knew, you'd not have come out of your city. You'd hide, you all would, because you'd be afraaaiiid."

A radio on the man's hip warbled. "Kenji, you got him?" a female voice asked.

Kenji fumbled with his weapon as he unclipped a device and held it to his mouth. The gun came up again. "I got this, Rocko. I got him. I got the law man, and Gabriel is going to be surprised. So surprised!"

"Quit screwing around and get him on the ground."

Miles took a breath and glanced at the hilltop and then at the nearest ridge. Movement. It wasn't much, and too far away for a target, not that he was armed, but he had a range of 180 meters to the sniper's location. He edged sidelong to his left, nearly placing Kenji between them.

"Hey!" Kenji said. "You! Hold still."

Miles squinted and lowered a hand slightly to shield his eyes. "Sorry. Sun's bright, and I'm feeling a bit wobbly after you shot the horse."

"Get down on the dirt."

"All right, no problem. You're in charge here. Can I call you Kenji?"

"No you can't, law man."

Rocko was moving, so Miles sidled further. "If it's good enough for Rocko, then why not me? I'm not a bad guy once we get to know each other."

"I said stop moving!"

"Kenji, you got this?" Rocko asked over the radio.

"Yeah, just stop distracting me!"

Miles took another step, his eyes locked on Kenji, but with a clear pin in his Insight display on where his partner was perched. Kenji was between him and Rocko. Wouldn't do Miles much good if Kenji blasted him. At such close range, how could the man miss?

In the corner of Miles' eye, Jaya shifted. Kenji was close enough. All he had to do was look in her direction and he'd see her legs.

"You got Ivan and Eddie," Miles said. "I'm just doing what my boss told me and making my patrols down here. They don't hear back from me, more marshals come. Talk to me, Kenji. Why are you and Rocko causing all this trouble? Why 'guilty'? What does that mean?"

"Get on the ground like I told you."

Miles eased himself to a knee. Burner too far away to grab. No handy rocks either. "So who's this Gabriel?"

That earned Kenji's upper lip two licks. "You'll see. You'll see soon enough."

"Maybe I met him already. Pleasant enough fellow, rides a white horse. Big backpack."

Kenji sneered. "You saw him because he wanted to be seen. But now we're going to get you where you'll meet him for real."

"Move aside!" Rocko called from the radio. "I can't see!"

"Don't worry, Kenji," Miles said. "You got this. Let's not accidentally shoot anyone, or Gabriel will be upset with all of us. That sound right?

We go to Manna, share a bottle of their finest mescal, hash out our problems like civil folk."

Kenji fumbled with the radio on his belt. "You don't know what you're in for, law man."

He unclipped the device. In that moment, his eye flickered and his coat caught, the gun hand wavering. With his metal fingers, Miles had clawed up a hard piece of clotted dirt. He flung it at Kenji while diving forward into the man's knees. The black pistol fired. Miles collided with the man and sent him down, landing on top of him, only to get clocked across the side of his head with the gun.

Kenji was screaming, the radio blaring as it fell. They tumbled, Miles trying to keep the man in check in case Rocko opened fire. But Kenji proved strong, forcing Miles' cybernetic arm back while trying to bring the pistol to bear. It was almost pointing at Miles, and another few centimeters would have the barrel at his throat.

Miles head-butted him.

Kenji jerked back, his arms losing their strength, the gun still in his grip. Miles twisted the man's wrist. The weapon fell. He tried to get Kenji under his control. Kenji slipped from his grip and squirmed away. Thunder rolled from the ridge above. The *whang* of a bullet ripping through the air. Miles imagined he could feel the heat off his backside as he sprang up. Kenji's pistol was in the wrong direction. He scrambled towards his dropped burner.

Gone.

Jaya had it and was waving him towards her. He leaped for the cover of rock and landed next to her. She pressed his weapon into his hand. He pointed the burner in Kenji's general direction and snapped off a few shots before taking cover.

A bullet atomized the top of the boulder next to Miles. He ducked further, catching his breath.

"You hit?" Jaya asked.

"Don't think so."

She uncurled herself and patted him down, but he pulled her close as another round pounded the dirt at their feet. A beige haze hovered around them. Where was Kenji? He fought to control his ragged breathing. Swallowed dust. Listened.

The last echoes of the rifle died away. His ears rang. All he could see was the dead horse and the long shadows of the rocks and the antenna.

Jaya clung to him. No tears, no shakes. She was visibly breathing hard, as if winded. "I hear him," she whispered.

"Coming closer?"

Shook her head. "Can't tell."

"Kenji?" Miles called. "You still there?"

Silence. Then, "That was a mistake, law man. A mistake. When Gabriel hears about this, he'll be angry."

"I wouldn't want that. Right now, your best bet is for you and Rocko to put down your weapons and surrender. More marshals will be here soon, and they'll have militia with them. Tanks. Guns. Armored troopers. What do you say we take care of this now and it'll go better for you?"

"Gabriel's gonna hear about this all right. And when he does, you'll be sorry. You'll wish you had stayed in Seraph."

"Way ahead of you, partner."

Chapter Sixteen

A cramp ran up Miles' left shoulder, his artificial right arm sending phantom pain signals that competed for attention.

The sun was setting, throwing an orange glow as the last of the light filtered through the pink clouds. The long shadows had grown wide until they enveloped the hilltop in twilight, yet Miles refused to move from cover, keeping Jaya in his grip. He fought the urge to reposition himself to ease the aches and numbness creeping along his legs. He worked his jaw repeatedly, trying to get his ears to stop reminding him of the gunshot that had exploded next to his head during his tussle with Kenji.

Over two hours had passed. Kenji hadn't called out again. He might have retreated, or he could be patiently waiting for Miles to stick his head out. Rocko could also be anywhere.

"Won't be totally dark for a couple of hours," Jaya whispered.

Sunset at 5:09 p.m., Insight prompted. *Moonrise at 9:19 p.m.*

Miles holstered his burner. "We can't stay here all night. I'm going to make a break for it. Might draw fire. If I do, run. Keep the rocks between you and any shooter. Get back to Manna and let Ruthie know what happened."

"You think you need to make a noble sacrifice on my behalf?"

"This is my job. You shouldn't have come with me."

She scoffed. "Caring for the town is my job, too."

"We can argue about it later. Splitting up means two targets. Better chance one of us makes it."

If his argument made sense to her, she didn't say. They waited for the last of the sun to vanish, and it grew dark quick.

"What's the chance they have a night scope?" she asked.

"Time to find out."

He half-stumbled as he ran while keeping hunkered down. Ignored the pins and needles. He passed the dead horse and rounded the rocks to the antenna. The track they had taken up the hill was the only one in sight. It would be hard enough to navigate; trying to find another way to the bottom of the ravine would result in a broken leg, neck, or both.

He took cover behind a wall of earth. Watched, listened, smelled. Kenji and Rocko probably hadn't been on foot.

Jaya scurried in his direction. She had recovered her satchel of supplies from the fallen horse. She huddled next to him.

"The plan was for us to split up," he said.

"Your plan. Mine is to not get killed getting back home. One way down, marshal."

The trail didn't have cover once they started their descent. Their jog soon turned into a lively strut. Near the base of the hill, they had plenty of boulders and a dry creek bed, but the path remained the most visible, a necessary evil if he wanted to get back to Manna without taking all night.

Jaya was limping. She brushed him off when he tried to help and refused to relinquish her pack.

"You're hurt," he said.

"When we came down off the horse. My ankle. I'll live."

The trail intersected a wider track that ran in two directions. Insight showed Miles had passed this way with the marshal and their prisoner, but there was no way to be certain in the dark. Jaya headed left. Miles followed. By the time the moon's pale glow appeared behind the clouds, they came to another fork.

She pointed to the left. He was about to follow when he spotted an askew sign on a metal post up the slope at the split in the road. Two arrows, both labeled. He took out his device and activated the screen. Repressed a sigh as he noticed a crack along the front of the phone, and the display wasn't showing anything but the light. With the faint screen illumination, he read the sign.

Manna and *Footsteps from Limbo.*

Arrows pointing right and left. Jaya wasn't taking them to Manna.

"This way," he said, and started walking down the split to the right.

She caught up with him. "You don't want to go that way."

"It's the way back to the camp. If I hadn't spotted that sign, you'd be leading me away. Why?"

The faint light caught the whites of her eyes as she looked up at him. "Because they'll kill you if you go back. We go to the next camp. It's tiny, but I know the family that runs it. They put us up, we get them to give us a ride to a north side trader's post where I'm sure you'll have a signal. Call for help. You get rescued. Your marshal friends can come tearing into Manna and see what's left."

"What's left? What do you mean? What's going to happen?"

"Something that's happened before down here. The desert takes care of her own. I lied when you asked about frontier justice. Those signs on Eddie and Ivan? They're judgments. This Gabriel is the judge. He and his followers show up every few years, and it's run or face trial. They say he sniffs out the guilty."

"Based on what?"

"Instinct. Telepathy. Who knows? The stories are crazy, and if you hadn't come into Manna when you did to tell us about Eddie, there'd be no warning."

Miles' jaw tightened as they walked. "Why are you telling me about this now?"

"You seem decent enough, Marshal Kim. But you're still a marshal. It's law first, humanity after. I've been on the receiving end of enough grief from marshals, Meridian security, or the Yellow Tigers to last a lifetime. And curse me, but I don't shed tears when I hear about a cop getting the tables turned by some scrapper trying to make ends meet out in the wastes. Going back to Manna now is suicide."

"You don't have to follow me. But tell me what I'm up against."

The hitch in her step had gotten worse, but she kept up. "It's rumors, mostly, because the old timers don't talk about it. Some sisters at prayer circle do, the younger ones anyway, when I get them alone. They've been through it before, and some welcome it. Gabriel's gang comes, they comb through the camp. Anyone accused of anything gets brought forward. Others get called out by the community. Gabriel has a list. The accused get a chance to plead their case, and then judgment."

"Murder."

"Not always. Rare, if that's to be believed. Might be a hand for a thief, or a beating, or banishment from camp. Anyone Gabriel sends away better keep running, from what I've heard. Enough folks fear him that they make themselves scarce."

"But this is all speculation. You heard they were coming?"

"I didn't. No one in my circle mentioned it. But seeing Eddie and Ivan...."

"How many people in his gang?" he asked.

"A dozen or more. Loyal and fanatic. Some think they were here before the return. Earthborn. Hate returnees as much as they do the Caretakers. Like you say, it's guesses. But it's not a mystery I care to solve."

"You have any specific reason to fear them?"

"Haven't you been listening? Everyone should be afraid."

A steaming pile of horse dung laid before them. Someone had either come or gone recently. Cool lights ahead marked Manna's thoroughfare.

Miles paused at a knee-high cinderblock wall that marked off a private garden next to one of the first homes. Checked his burner for the tenth time. Its reassuring weight on his hip didn't help with the fluttering in his gut. Besides the main drag, the rest of the camp was dark. The night before saw many of the shanties illuminated by cooking fires and lamplight, but now the terraces felt devoid of life.

"I'm going to go on ahead," he said. "You need to hide here and stay out of sight."

Jaya had been clutching her pack to keep the contents from rattling. "I can check and see what's going on. They were after you, not me."

"Someone rode into town recently. Want to bet it was Kenji or Rocko or both? If you show up, they'll know I'm here."

She nodded. He left her by the wall and scurried from shadow to shadow.

The brightest lights came from the front of the bar. Six horses were hitched at a rail out front, with three figures under an overhang. There were people inside, but Miles only caught glimpses. Some were armed.

He rose for a better look but ducked back behind the corner of a shack as a mother with two children hurried towards the bar and vanished inside. The mother hushed her children. Then she pulled something over each one's face before fixing one to her own. Bandanas? Masks? Was she afraid of spreading germs?

Zooming in with his right eye, he saw the face coverings of the children were brightly painted cloth. But the mother's was hard plastic or wood, likewise decorated with a design he couldn't make out. Others in the bar wore masks too, a simple bag with holes, an over-the-eyes party mask, and even protective face shields worn for sports or something he expected from a tactical loadout.

A gang member paced into view. No mask. Dark hat, greasy hair, a week's worth of stubble. His eyes were on the crowd.

While the gathering was mostly silent, murmuring and whispering, Miles saw the type of elbow nudges and fidgeting of a group of people waiting for something exciting to happen. Like a show was about to start. Or church, if that was their poison.

They wanted to be there.

He'd have to be careful. It wasn't just Gabriel and his gang he'd have to watch out for. If the good people of Manna feared their visitors, they'd be likely to report an unwelcome marshal prowling about.

He needed to get to Jodie and Walker and get them out of town. They had the prospects of stealing horses, although riding at night might make for a very brief getaway. But perhaps the gang had a car.

Cutting through the back lots of several homes, he made his way to a path that led towards Ruthie's terrace. Horses coming. A pair of riders trotted down the lantern-lit street. Miles took cover beneath an overhang where sheets and a blanket were strewn along a laundry line. A water barrel sat beneath a drainpipe fed by the rain gutters along the roof of a shoebox-shaped home.

The mounts snuffled as they clopped by. The riders were silent. Miles' boot kicked a pot half-filled with water, and it clattered and spilled. One rider turned his direction. White horse. Enough light caught the lines of his hat and his slender face. It was the man they had encountered on the road before discovering Ivan's body at the antenna array and getting ambushed.

Miles crouched in complete shadow, absolutely still, but it felt like the man on the white horse was staring straight at him. But the two kept going and vanished on the thoroughfare, heading towards the bar.

No one else was in the narrow lane, with no signs of life in any of the homes. Was the bar big enough to accommodate everyone? He doubted it. Hadn't Jaya said that some leave camp if they knew this Gabriel was coming?

He broke cover and jogged.

A curtain at a nearby shack moved. Someone had shut it just as Miles passed. One resident was still home and in hiding.

A light up ahead. A blue halogen hand lamp, like something from a mechanic's garage, hung from a hook outside Ruthie's home. Miles squinted as he approached, the light blinding and creating shapes and shadows from the porch furniture and decorations.

Ruthie reclined in one of the large wooden chairs. She held a bottle between thumb and forefinger. Her red hair hung everywhere. She spat when Miles appeared.

"Thought they got you," she slurred.

"Where's Marshal Jodie?"

Ruthie waved vaguely at the ajar front door. Miles hurried past her and went inside. The home's interior only had a few recessed accent lights on, making navigating the cluttered space precarious, but he found his way to the back bedroom and found a light switch.

Marshal Jodie was still in bed, his sweaty body mostly uncovered. His mouth hung open and his eyes were closed. Miles placed a hand on his chest. Still breathing.

"He's fine," Ruthie said. Miles hadn't noticed her following him. "He was even awake earlier. Took some broth. Said he had a headache and his guts were burning, but he's alive."

"Gabriel's gang..."

"Yeah. They're here. And you know about them now. What happened out there?"

"They must have gotten to Eddie. Found a 'guilty' sign where they had strung him up. Looks like they killed your man Ivan, too."

She took a swig. "Ivan should have left."

"You knew they were coming? Why didn't you warn him? Why didn't you warn us?"

"Because this isn't Seraph. And Gabriel coming is not new news. He's always coming. He doesn't exactly keep a schedule of his rounds. We get rumors. He might show up in a week, in a month, and I keep hoping never again, but he always does."

"So why don't you do something about it? Jodie and I are here. We could have called for help. Now we're cut off."

"They never did that before. I've only been here for two of Gabriel's visits. He holds court, scares a few people, beats a few of the accused down. Always warning about what will happen for those who don't repent. This thing with Ivan and your man at High Spring...it's different from the other times. Heard about him executing people, but always dismissed it, figuring it was just talk."

"Two dead isn't talk. They shot our horse."

Ruthie's face clouded over. "Where'd you get a horse?"

"It was Jaya's. She was with me. They sniped at us, and we managed to get off the hill after sundown."

"I thought I told you to stay away from her."

"She offered to come with me. I wasn't going to refuse. Is that still the issue? Seems like you've got more to worry about in your camp than a flighty medic. What's going to happen here?"

She tilted her bottle, but it was empty. She set it next to the bed and got Marshal Jodie sitting up. His eyes fluttered and he moaned. "I get you two out of here."

"Not just us. Where's Walker?"

"Gabriel was asking about him. Doesn't sound good. Tell me where he is, and I'll do what I can. But this is your opportunity. Get out of camp. Keep moving. The east trail will take you to a wadi you can follow north. There's a spring on the way, and if you don't rest too much, you'll make it to a scrapper camp where there's a delivery dog station."

He assisted Jodie with his boots. Jodie stayed upright and pulled on his clothing with a little help. Once Miles got him standing, Jodie gave him a nod.

"You can show us this east trail out of camp?" Miles asked Ruthie.

"We move fast and leave now. I'll give you a couple of canteens I have filled."

She had the canteens ready in the kitchen and followed them out. When she tried to hand them to Miles, he didn't take them.

"Don't be stupid," she said. "You'll need these. I can't go with you. I have my responsibilities."

"Might be a little late to start caring about what happens to the people in your camp. You get Marshal Jodie to the trail. I'll find you once I collect Walker. Then you can come back home and drown yourself with that swill."

Jodie groaned. "What are you doing, Kim? Forget Walker. Let's get out of here. I'm the senior marshal, remember? We take the trail out of camp and come back with reinforcements."

"We leave Walker, we find another body."

"He's not worth it."

"You're probably right. But that's what I'm doing."

Ruthie had Jodie leaning on her arm. "This isn't the deal."

"It is for me. Walker's our prisoner and our responsibility. I'm bringing him out of here alive."

Ruthie glared at him. For a moment, he thought she might try something. She said, "If you can find Dora, tell her where I went."

"I will."

She nodded and assisted Marshal Jodie to the front porch. She switched the lamp off and they headed up the terrace, leaving Miles alone to return to the camp to find his prisoner.

Chapter Seventeen

Miles' boots crunched too loudly on the gravel lot near the main intersection of camp. Solar panels in a side lot provided cover, so it was the best way to remain out of sight. A trickle of residents on the street beyond passed him by, and none appeared to notice him.

They, too, were heading for the bar.

A horse snorted up ahead. Someone stood next to it, but in the shadows, their details remaining obscured. Miles glimpsed a red light in their hands, something small, like a power indicator or some other device. They were sweeping what was in their hands before them at eye level. Infrared, thermal scope, or some other sensor? They appeared to be scanning a cottage on the opposite side of the street.

So the gang used tech. He crouched behind a transformer box to watch the sentry. Miles needed to get past him to make it to the path leading up to where the guest tent waited.

The sentry whistled. Another figure appeared in the dark and vanished into the cottage. A man squealed, protested, struggled as the gang brought him outside. He wore tattered pants and a blazer missing an arm. The gang member marched him along down towards the bar.

Not everyone wanted to be present for Gabriel's extravaganza.

Ruthie hadn't known where her sister was. Had she also missed the fact Dora and Walker were together? He had to hope they had successfully hidden from the gang. If they were just starting their sweep, then maybe Dora and Walker were still where Miles had left them.

It wasn't too late to grab Jaya and slink back to Ruthie's and try to find the east path out of Manna.

The guard with the sensor was making a circle now and stopped when he pointed his device in Miles' direction.

Too late to run.

Miles broke from cover and walked towards him. "Sorry, I was running late."

The guard lowered the device and stared at Miles. He wore a pistol on his hip.

Miles punched him, a metal fist to the solar plexus. The scanner went tumbling. The man staggered and gasped as Miles stepped close and delivered a wallop to his gut. Miles eased him to the ground before dropping to a knee. The sentry clawed at him. Miles hit him a few more times until the man went limp. He rolled the man onto his stomach and used his victim's belt to bind his wrists. The man groaned. Miles patted him down. Found a handkerchief to serve as a gag. Took off the weapon belt. He dragged the man to the shadows by the transformer and left him there.

He recovered the scanner and inspected it.

An electromagnetic wave sensor. Could hear people breathing, see them moving, and detect a heartbeat through walls. Miles scanned it about and saw another local tucked away behind a chicken coop next to five birds hunkered on a perch. No way to know how many more of the devices the gang might possess, but they didn't have this one. But using it would prove to be a distraction.

He crushed the device with the heel of his boot.

While he wanted to question the sentry, he heard voices approaching. Three, maybe four people coming. Insight wanted to target them. While an ambush might work, they didn't sound like they were bunched up, and the street provided ample cover. This wasn't the place for a shootout. Regular slugs could punch holes through the buildings, and too many locals might get hurt. The gang's numbers meant he'd quickly find himself surrounded.

He left the sentry lying in the shadows and hurried up the path towards the guest tent.

The tent stood empty. "Paxton?" He listened for a moment. "Dora?" Miles checked the first tent where they had spent part of the night. They weren't there, either. Shouldn't have stomped the sensor.

A gunshot echoed. Close by. He crouched and strained his ears and eyes. From up ahead, a dog barked. Not any dog, *his* dog.

Miles ran. A yurt stood at a corner of the lane next to a goat pen. The animals were clustered to one side of the enclosure. The dog stood at the entrance of the yurt, hackles up, and frothing as he snarled at a gang member who appeared to be trying to get past him to get inside.

"Just shoot it, Rocko," Kenji said. He stood backed up to a water cistern and was cradling his arm. A knocked-over lantern lay at his feet.

Rocko was having trouble with her rifle, a bolt operated slug thrower. "I did. That's one tough dog."

She had dropped one cartridge on the ground and was fumbling with another when Miles shot her. Kenji dove for the rifle when Miles shot him, too. Both lay groaning in the dirt.

Eighty-nine percent median chance their wounds aren't fatal.

"Oddly specific, Insight." He approached his dog. The artificial animal was panting, his tongue out. A starburst of blood marked its left flank. Tail tucked and ears down, he came forward and whined.

Miles stroked his head. "Where's Walker, boy?"

The dog was licking his hand. Laser fire and two injured people moaning? Someone doubtlessly heard.

To the yurt, he called, "It's Marshal Kim. Anyone in there?"

"Marshal?" Paxton Walker said from inside. "I need help."

Miles pushed the blanket serving as a door aside and entered, weapon up. It was too dark to see clearly, but the lantern outside provided just enough light to spot a table thrown on its side and a hunkered shape quivering behind it.

"Walker? We need to leave. Now."

"She's hurt."

Miles rounded the table. Dora lay sprawled out on the floor, a piece of rebar clutched in one hand. She had two darts in her, one in her chest and another in her shoulder.

Walker held her shotgun. "They...those savages ordered her to surrender me to them. She fought them. She didn't go down. We made it here when she was overcome by whatever is on those things. I didn't dare to take them out. I didn't know if I should. I...what do we do?"

"Why didn't you shoot them?"

Walker looked at his weapon as if he had forgotten it was there. "It wasn't loaded."

Miles crouched next to Dora. She was breathing. When he placed a hand on a dart, her eyes fluttered open. They were crusted and bloodshot.

"Don't touch them," Dora rasped. "They hurt. Ahh!"

He tugged the dart out of her shoulder. "We're in trouble and I need to get those out."

"Can't move. Where's my sister?"

"Ruthie took Marshal Jodie and they left. We get going before any of the gang catches up."

He pulled at the dart in her chest. It resisted until he wiggled it and got it free. Dora gritted her teeth and was breathing heavy. Foamy spit rolled from her mouth, and snot trickled down her nose.

Miles waved Walker over. "Get under her shoulder."

Dora shoved him. It was a weak push, but enough to get his attention. "You were supposed to find out what happened to Eddie."

"I'll explain it as we move. The gang won't wait."

"Tell me. Everything."

"He was hit by a dart like these. Paralyzed. Strung up above the spring with a guilty sign. Might have died of exposure, or had enough strength to get himself free before falling. I'm sorry."

"He was a bad man. But he was mine."

"Now let's get you to your feet."

She pointed the piece of rebar at him. "This is my camp. I'm not leaving."

"Your sister doesn't have a problem getting out."

"My sister is the smart one. I don't care about you marshals; she does. You did your part and told me about Eddie. Now leave me alone."

"My sister is the smart one. I don't care about you marshals; she does. You did your part and told me about Eddie. Now leave me alone."

Chapter Eighteen

Kenji and Rocko remained where Miles had left them on the ground outside the yurt. No one else appeared to be coming, but the conversation with Dora had taken too long. He removed the pistol from the gun belt he had taken from the first sentry and tossed the belt aside.

Walker held out his hand. "Good, marshal. With both of us armed, we'll be formidable. They won't stop us."

"Not a chance," Miles said as he tucked the pistol into his belt. "Keep your voice down."

Miles searched Kenji, but he had no weapons. Besides the rifle, Rocko was likewise unarmed. Miles examined the rifle for a moment. It could fire a variety of cartridges. It also had a thumbprint safety. Worthless to him. He fumbled with it for a moment before removing the bolt and flinging it into the night, rendering the weapon useless.

"He'll get you, law man," Kenji wheezed.

A faint crackle garbled from Rocko. A radio, he realized. He unclipped an earpiece and throat mike he had missed before and pressed it to his ear.

"...where you at?" a gruff voice asked. "Going to start soon. Rocko?"

Miles put the earpiece on but muted the microphone. Had no one heard the laser fire?

Walker shifted on his feet, a rabbit ready to bolt.

"There's an east trail out of camp," Miles said. "It's that way."

"What about a car or a horse? My feet hurt."

A quick check confirmed both Kenji and Rocko had shoes that were too small for Walker.

"It's walk or stay," Miles said. "The trail is past the last of the homes. Marshal Jodie is up there waiting. Get moving."

"You want me to go alone? There's more of those animals, if you hadn't noticed."

"I noticed. But I also left the nurse behind, and I have to go get her. Head to the end of the road here and wait. If you see any of them coming, run. They'll find you if you hide. Take my dog with you."

"There's something weird about your canine."

"From the look of it, he probably saved your life. I'll catch up once I find Jaya."

He crouched next to the dog. The animal snuffled and nuzzled Miles' face. *Just a machine*, he reminded himself. He patted him gently, his hand softly probing the wound on the dog's side.

"Go with Walker. I'll come get you."

The dog had his ears perked up as Miles went to leave. Miles expected the animal might follow him and he'd have to lock him up. But then Walker hurried off, and the dog scampered after him.

Miles returned towards the center of camp alone.

Jaya wasn't waiting at the wall where he had left her. He whispered her name, circled around the back of the nearest huts, and cursed having destroyed the sentry's device. Looking through homes might be useful.

He didn't encounter anyone else on the streets of the camp. A buzz carried from the bar, the earlier silence replaced by an excited murmur.

The chatter on the radio piped up once more. "Rocko, I need to hear from you. Is Kenji with you? We have a man down."

Miles had taken a set of makeshift stairs to a cul-de-sac that let out onto the main road, bypassing the solar array where he had left the downed sentry. The gang knew something was wrong. They'd be searching soon, and Kenji remained conscious and would undoubtedly make noise to summon help.

"We're starting," a voice boomed from a loudspeaker inside the bar.

He knew he should leave. Take the same route back to the cul-de-sac, join Walker, and regroup with Marshal Jodie and Ruthie. Jaya said she hadn't been worried about herself. But even she had admitted her knowledge of what the gang did during their raids was based on rumor.

"I see you, settlers, citizens, and brethren," the voice continued. "Some of you span generations here; others are new. The breath of our dead lives on in the scrub and grass of the desert. To the south, the jungles once again thrive. The forests to the north return, clawing back at the ground poisoned by neglect. All bear witness to those of us who would nurture our home, our world, back to health. But she is sick, oh so sick."

A rumble of agreement from the crowd packed inside the bar. And the voice? It was the man he and Jaya had encountered on their way towards High Spring.

The loudspeaker crackled. "I am Gabriel. Some know me. Most of you have heard of me. We bring justice. Not the powerless, corrupt authority from Seraph, but the righteous law of Earth and Heaven. The old ways were left behind by those who despoiled our world. Then they dare try to reclaim it as if it belonged to them. See the sights of the town to the north. Have you seen it? The rubbish-strewn filth? The pollution? The ground is not yet healed, yet it once again bleeds. And why? Because they allow themselves to be ruled by the same ones who brought on the dawn of our thousand years of blight, yet run back into its bosom. Why? Money, comfort, the things sweet to the tongue despite the bitterness to the soul."

Miles took position behind a broken hulk of a dirt mover. He was a couple of buildings down, with a fresh vantage point. He counted seven horses instead of six, now that he had a clear view of the side alley. The seventh was Gabriel's milky white horse.

Three gang members were positioned out front, with one at the alley entrance. He spotted Jaya. She was just inside the side doorway, positioned behind Tanni in her wheelchair and Horace the barkeeper. Both were wearing face coverings, Jaya's mask a simple red scarf drawn up over her mouth and nose and Tanni's a grimacing devil's face of violet and red with bared fangs.

He pulled out his own bandana as Gabriel continued with his sermon. The cloth around his nose and mouth wouldn't fool anyone who looked at him. The side of his face and his right eye would need a full helmet to conceal, and his dress and sidearm were an instant giveaway. But the crowd was transfixed, and the gang members were likewise intent on the service.

"Justice," Gabriel said. "Punishment for the guilty. Release for the innocent. A balm for the victims, and a unifier to a people who no longer wish to be lost."

Miles cut across the street, pausing at the corner near the horses. His heart hammered. What was Jaya thinking? Why hadn't she run? She was out of whispering range. He edged his way into the alley, willing the nearest gang member to continue paying attention to Gabriel's blathering.

Gabriel stood on the bar. "Some call me a judge. But that's *all* our responsibility. What I do is find the guilty. It is you who passes judgment. Let us begin."

Applause and a few whoops. A commotion rose as someone tried to get up and push his way out of the bar, only to be brought back to his seat by a gang member. He wore a blazer missing an arm. It was the man who had been flushed out earlier by the sentry with the sensor.

"No, no, no!" the man cried. "I don't want to be here."

"Then you should have run this morning when you heard Gabriel was coming!" a shrill woman in a hooded mask shouted.

"Should have thought of that before you stole the charger off my roof," a man out of the line of sight added.

"Thief!" another shouted.

Miles made it to the alley doorway. The sentry was in reach, but taking him down wasn't possible without half the bar seeing.

"An accusation of theft," Gabriel said. "Would anyone else share an accusation?"

"He took a box of food bars from my pantry while I was out trading," an elderly woman in a dog mask said.

"Witnesses?"

"Wrappers in his rubbish pile."

"That's not true!" the accused man cried. "I found the food on a busted-down delivery dog."

Gabriel crouched and beckoned to the guard. "Bring him."

The guard moved the struggling man towards Gabriel. Gabriel turned off the microphone fixed to his collar and reached for the man. The accused moaned and trembled as Gabriel drew him into an embrace and whispered soft words that Miles couldn't hear.

Then, as gentle as a parting lover, Gabriel gazed at the accused. "Guilty."

Two of the camp dwellers had come up behind the man and took him, forcing him to the floor.

"Two fingers. One for the theft. The other for the lies."

The man screamed, but the cry was muffled as a gag was forced into his mouth. The guard handed a large blade to one of the camp dwellers. Miles had his hand on the butt of his weapon. Was breathing too hard. Two of the guards from out front had entered the bar and had their own weapons out, surveying the crowd. He lowered his head, hoping his hat brim would obscure his face. But then he stepped forward, only to be stopped by Jaya.

She had backed up next to him and now had a hand on his. Glanced up at him. Shook her head. Breathed, "No."

Insight was winking for his attention. He dismissed the notifications. This was the wrong time for a phantom update to a Meridian server he had no access to.

Another of the camp dwellers had joined the other two in subduing the struggling man. With their masks on, it was like the scene from a freakish pantomime. Clowns, demons, laughing crones, rough-spun sacks with eyeholes. The crowd had grown still.

Gabriel remained crouched, watching, his face serene. When the woman in the dog mask who had charged the accused man of stealing food laughed, Gabriel glared at her.

"No!" Gabriel said. "We don't rejoice. What we do is grievous. But it yields peaceable fruitage. We discipline and administer justice so that we teach ourselves to never stray again."

The accused man shrieked. One of the camp dwellers had borne down with the knife, leaned back as if to appraise his work, and then went in again. The cries of the accused continued for a moment before they let the man go, leaving him quivering on the wooden planks, clutching at his bloody hand. Two fingers lay beside him.

It was Jaya who rushed forward. She kneeled beside the man and pressed a thick square of gauze on the oozing wounds. It took her a moment and she needed help, but they got the man back to his seat, where he sagged.

Miles stayed fixed in place, the horror of the scene replaying in his mind. Was this but the first of more acts of brutality? What was his option? Draw his burner and try to put a stop to the obscenity of justice? They had gone after Marshal Jodie. He feared Gabriel and his followers wouldn't back down and wouldn't hesitate to open fire inside the crowded bar.

Gabriel stood up again and turned on his microphone. "Receive your neighbor back joyfully. Let us continue. Who else brings an accusation? Anyone?"

The crowd was silent. Whatever enthusiasm had come before the mutilation was gone. Gabriel stepped down from the bar and went to the second row of chairs. Leaned close to a woman with straight brown hair and wearing a smiling wooden clown mask with faded paint.

"You came with an accusation in your heart," Gabriel said. "Where is it now?" When she hesitated, he purred, "What would you bring before us? What requires justice? Speak it."

"My husband. He cheated on me."

Gabriel looked at the man next to her. "A charge of adultery has been laid before us."

The man tore off his mask and stood. Tears streamed down his face. "I told you, Linda, I was sorry. It was ten years ago. Ten years. And just once!"

"Guilty," Gabriel whispered.

"It was just once," the man sobbed. "We made peace over this. She said she forgave me."

"But this isn't the only indiscretion, is it?"

"W-what? I didn't...never again. It's over."

"Marital infidelity is not what we punish. While sad, these are matters left to a family to work out. But community justice requires us to respect one another. I sense anger in both of you. For the next thirty days, you may not speak to each other. At the end of this time, you will either reconcile, or separate."

The husband and wife looked at him, looked at each other, and the husband sat down.

Miles remained on edge. Was that it? He had been expecting a violent penalty like the severing of fingers over a theft.

Gabriel moved onto the third row. Someone confessed to having moved a fence marker. He was brought to the center aisle, stripped naked, and beaten with sticks by his neighbors.

A woman tearfully admitted to having poisoned a neighbor's dog who barked too much. The neighbor wasn't present, having passed away a few years prior. Gabriel ordered her to return home and take a purgative.

Gabriel appeared to have a sense of who was holding back. He sought them out, and there were more tears and confessions of lies, accusations of neglect, sloth, and shoddy craft in the camp carpenter's home repairs. These were resolved by neighbors slapping neighbors, hot metal pressed to shoulders, and a thumb broken by a frying pan, respectively.

The group of masked camp dwellers helped the inept carpenter with the pulped thumb back to his seat.

Miles kept his runaway breathing under control. No more severed limbs. No one was getting strung up. He dared hope this would be the worst the camp would endure.

"Justice leaves the past behind and brings us into the present," Gabriel said. "Nothing here is hidden. A moment of pain, and then release and a clean conscience. For those who believe, a road to reconciliation with the Divine. Your camp will be stronger for it. Your community refreshed. Who else has a matter of justice? Who else wishes to unburden themselves?"

Jaya had her patient sitting up on his own strength. Miles tried to catch her eye. *Time to leave.* He edged forward, willing her to turn her head. He bumped into Tanni's wheelchair.

She looked up at him, her devil mask leering. "Here, Gabriel! I have a matter! This is one of the Seraph marshals, and he's guilty as sin."

Chapter Nineteen

Miles drove his elbow into the face of the guard next to him. The man hit his head against the doorframe on the way down. Miles disarmed him, pulling the man's slung short-barrel shotgun away and pointing it at Gabriel.

Gabriel walked slowly towards him as the crowd gasped and cowered. His gang had their weapons pointing in Miles' direction. While Insight painted targets, the shotgun was the wrong tool for the situation, and there were too many people in the way. The software in his head kept nagging at him.

Not now.

"You're Marshal Kim," Gabriel said. "Set the weapon down. You see your situation? Outnumbered, unwelcome, an intruder representing an institution with no authority here."

Clearing his throat, Miles tried for his best authoritative voice. "This is Seraph territory. This tribunal of yours is unlawful. It ends now."

Gabriel shook his head. "Or? You don't know, do you? Shoot me and prove your law stands above us? You could try. What you see here is the people's justice. This camp decides to carry out this court's decisions."

"Murder and maiming aren't my idea of justice."

"Except when it serves you."

"This isn't a debate. Order your people to set their weapons down. You attacked a marshal. And then there's...this."

Gabriel frowned and he nodded slowly. "Your words make me sad. I heard what happened to Marshal Jodie. I understand it was an accident."

"I don't care that you have hurt feelings. We'll figure out the rest later. Weapons down. Hands up."

"You have no say in the lives of these souls, marshal. This camp renounces your law. What I will allow is for you to leave Manna with your life. All I ask in return is you leave your prisoner with us."

"Paxton Walker? What do you want with him?"

"You heard what we do here. I resolve matters of justice. And Mr. Walker is known to us."

Miles was about to ask more when he became distracted. While Gabriel kept his eyes locked on him, several faces in the audience glanced at the doorway behind Miles. Someone in the alley was moving his way. One of the outside guards appeared, using the white horse as cover. He raised a weapon.

Miles dove under the bar as automatic fire sent a dozen rounds through the tent. People were screaming. The bar had no cover. He elbow-crawled through the back tent flap as the town's residents hit the floor. Miles found a place behind a stack of crates full of bottles. Liquor splashed down from a crate struck by bullets. He ditched the shotgun and drew his burner.

A quick glimpse, and Insight began processing as he ducked back into cover.

Gabriel was nowhere in sight. A dozen people were trying to get out the main door. Two of the guards were at the front. Targeted with red squares now. But he couldn't see the side door or the man with the submachine gun. Miraculously, he didn't see anyone who appeared to have been struck by the barrage.

A few meters away, Jaya huddled next to a group of camp residents. They might as well have a chasm between them. There was no safe way for her to come to him. He could only hope she was as safe as anyone else in Manna.

Gabriel shouted from somewhere, "Go around back!"

Miles would be surrounded. Even with Insight targeting, there was no way he'd get out of the fight alive, and between shotguns and automatic weapons, the bar would turn into a massacre.

He was up and running. Out the back, the way was clear as he sprinted for a drainage ditch that ran along the rear of the row of the nearest structures. The staccato bursts of gunfire made him dive into the concrete gutter.

"He's here! He's—"

In a single motion, Miles popped over the lip of the trench and shot the silhouette of one of the gang members standing in plain sight. Same man who had been at the side of the bar, a boxy black weapon dropping from his hands. The man yelped and crumpled.

Miles was wishing for the shotgun again as he sprang to his feet and ran.

The calling voices played tricks on his sense of direction.

He thought he was running for the stairway that would lead him to the terrace, but found himself at a dead end with a fire ring of metal and a rubbish heap. A vertical wall of earth enclosed the blind alley.

Beyond the nearest row of shacks, bright beams of white light sliced through the night. His breathing was already coming hard, and a cramp ran down his side. The stench of spoiled foodstuffs permeated the dumping site, and while there was cover, he didn't want to die there.

On top of it all, Insight kept blinking the minimized warnings. Had he been wounded? Didn't think so. If his module was about to crash, he could only hope it would leave the rest of him functioning.

He clambered past the gutted shell of an excavator. No matter where he placed himself, unless they came at him one at a time and out in the open, he'd get pinned down, and it would be only a matter of time before someone shot him.

The arm of the excavator made the machine look like a half-buried man with their fist in the dirt. While the angle was steep, it might be climbable. He surveyed the cliff. The lip was five meters above him and a couple of meters from the old machine's arm. Jumpable on a good day, in daylight, with a younger body or one with enhancements below the waistline.

He climbed.

The excavator arm was slick from the drizzle, but there were enough edges to find fingerholds. At the elbow, he stopped. It was the highest point, and the rest of the arm was at too steep of an angle.

Flashlight beams began sweeping the dump site.

Two targets, walking closer. Miles didn't dare let go with his hand, but couldn't move, either. Jumping and landing would make noise. He fought to calm his breathing. Reaffirmed his grip with his left hand so he could draw the burner.

They checked the refuse piles, walking around them, and played the light about around the bottom of the excavator. From his perch, he couldn't miss. Head shots, most likely, but then Miles realized both of the people with the flashlights wore masks. They were camp residents, not gang members. Neither had a weapon.

He kept the target on them as he willed them to keep moving, to see nothing, to go back home and pray for the night to end for them all.

One of them shined their light up at him.

Miles pointed his weapon. "Drop the flashlights and get out of here."

They set their lights down and ran. Their shouting voices were calling for help. Miles holstered the burner. Someone with a gun would show up soon.

Time to jump.

He leaped for the ledge, his body slamming on the rough packed dirt with both hands scrambling to find a purchase even as his feet kicked at the air. Gravel and clots of ground came loose as he clawed, finally gripping something that didn't give. He crawled forward, drawing his legs up, and trembled for a moment before standing. The rough-hewn wall had enough of a ledge that he could ease his way to where the terrace lane began.

Shouts, hoots, and more lights were coming from below. Unless they saw him jump, he had bought himself an extra moment or two. There were no signs of life ahead. He took the chance and started running down the center of the terrace, navigating the clutter. The shanties here were pressed close enough to have their roofs almost touch.

While the camp neighborhood was dark, it wasn't completely vacant. A baby was crying from one house with a canvas roof. A head peered out and ducked back in as Miles raced past.

"Stay inside," Miles called. "Lock your doors."

But he had no way of helping the people of Manna. He needed to make it to the eastern trail.

Chatter on the stolen radio. "Who's got eyes on the town? Anyone?"

"Negative," a second voice answered. "Rocko's down."

"Carmine? Report in. You up at the overlook?"

A third voice, a woman's. Carmine? "Heading there now."

Static. A crumpling sound like the one giving orders was shaking his mike around inside a plastic bag. "You're supposed to stay up there."

"Wanted to see the show," Carmine said.

"Gabriel's going to be pissed."

"You're going to tell him?"

"Of course I'm going to tell him. Because he'll know."

"Hey, Top?" the second voice said. "Rocko's alive, but her radio's gone."

"Okay, everyone. Switch to backup channel."

The radio went silent. The exchange had told him enough. The gang had tech and knew how to use it, and had enough forethought to have a backup radio frequency. They also had at least one watcher out in an elevated vantage point who was even now returning to her position. How many minutes before Carmine made it back up to this overlook?

Miles realized he wasn't certain where he was. A few shacks were up on a higher terrace, and he had lost all sense of direction. Insight kept telling him he had indeed been jogging east, but he had the distinct feeling he was on a street unknown to him.

He stopped. Caught his breath. Searched the homes for anything he might recognize that would orient him. Blathering speech came from somewhere below and slightly behind him. Husky, feminine, with no attempt at trying to keep quiet.

Dora?

Had she recovered enough to make it to the center of camp?

Walking carefully as to not accidentally kick or knock anything over, he backtracked. Between two of the huts was an almost invisible alleyway with stone steps that ran down towards the street below. Dora's hulking silhouette leaned against a second, equally imposing figure. Ruthie.

"Get me home," Dora was saying.

Ruthie groaned with the strain of keeping her sister upright. "I'm taking you to the clinic and getting you checked out."

"No. I'm fine."

A flashlight beam opposite Miles caught both sisters in a blazing corona.

"Get that light out of my eyes or I'll break your neck," Ruthie said.

The light beam didn't waver. "Everyone is supposed to be at the bar," the gang member said. It was the commanding voice they called Top from the radio. "Even you, Ruthie. Gabriel's orders."

Miles pressed himself against the sheet metal wall of the nearest hut, trying to stay out of the halo of light.

"Can't you see my sister's sick?" Ruthie said.

Top played the light between the two Alcott sisters. "We have sentries who were attacked. What happened to her?"

"Get out of my way, little man."

Miles squinted. He drew his weapon but had no shot. He realized there were more gang members at the bottom of the stairway. Ruthie's sidearm was slung. Dora no longer had her rebar.

When Ruthie took another step down, Top shouted, "Stop. Raise your hands, both of you."

A second flashlight beam was on them now, along with other hazy shapes impossible to make out. Miles adjusted his grip on his burner. The stairway went up and down and appeared to connect with another terrace. If that was where Ruthie and Dora had come from, it would take Miles where he needed to go.

Was Carmine even now climbing into place at her overwatch and eyeing the camp through a thermal scope?

With the standoff, Miles was stuck.

"The Alcott Sisters," Gabriel said from below in a resplendent tone.

"Daughters of storm giants. The leaders of Manna. We missed you tonight."

"Tell your men to stand down. My sister's hurt."

"So it seems. But why was she fighting with my disciples?"

"She was drunk."

"Don't insult me. She was hit by a tranquilizer, wasn't she? You promised cooperation. Yet I have four men injured or dead. You've exploited my forbearance."

"And you nearly ruined everything by having that idiot sniper of yours shoot the marshal."

"Ruthie, sweet Ruthie. You still try to hold back information from me. Manna had not one but two marshals visiting. And the fugitive who was here is gone."

"Your deal wasn't with me. I let you come here and do your thing. Same with the marshals. Leave me out of your ritual. I'm not picking sides."

"Deception and acts of omission *is* picking a side. You'd be party to Seraph and her corruption? Where are the marshals?"

"Does it look like I know? Move out of the way. I'm taking my sister—"

A sharp *crack-crack-crack* exploded up the alley as Ruthie and Dora Alcott fell.

"Guilty," Gabriel announced. "Finish them."

A gang member with a flashlight advanced on the fallen pair, a pistol aimed and prepared for the coup de grâce.

Miles fired.

The sentry yelped as the burner beam hit him center mass. The other lights vanished as the gang members scrambled for cover.

"He's here! The marshal's here!" a woman shouted from a rooftop above him.

Miles was backing up the stairs. He discharged his weapon in the gang's direction. He had no targets, no lights, and no one was sticking their head out. When his burner ran dry, he turned and bounded towards the high terrace.

Chapter Twenty

An itch ran down Miles' spine as he rushed past home after home, trying his best to duck under every canopy and overhang and weave and do everything in his power to make himself a hard target for anyone aiming at him.

Insight still blinked for his attention. No time for that now.

If the gang's overwatch had an aim assist and implants, all his footwork would make little difference. If they had a rifle that fired smart projectiles, he'd be dead. But Manna had grown silent since the brief firefight that had taken down the Alcott sisters and one more gang member.

He knew they were in pursuit.

All he had to do was get himself out of the camp and find Marshal Jodie and their fugitive so they could run, on foot, through a desert canyon while being chased by a homicidal cult obsessed with an arbitrary and archaic code of law, who would be even now getting their horses and coming after him.

Easy.

The tingle in the back of his head doubled down. It was now raw, pulsing electricity. The phantom sensation was every instinct telling him to take cover. But Manna had no defensible positions. The gang had the high ground, snipers, and enough people to surround even the biggest of the patchwork houses in the camp. They also had automatic firearms and possibly other weapons in their arsenal. One grenade could take down a row of the flimsy shanties. And the bad luck souls who might be cowering inside would suffer.

Leaving was the only option. It meant placing himself in potential line-of-sight for a sniper. But that didn't mean he had to make it easy.

While he hadn't taken time to slap a fresh battery pack in his spent burner, he could target. Insight would let him know of any laser tracker. None so far.

As his lungs burned and his muscles threatened to lock up, he stumbled past the last of the homes and another rubbish pit to a hillock of sandstone where a worn path ran up to a crest. He climbed, fell, and scuttled over, finding himself sliding in loose gravel down the opposite slope.

The moon hung behind a bank of clouds, throwing out enough light to make out shapes before him.

"Kim?" Marshal Jodie called.

Miles raised his hands. "Don't shoot. Yeah, Jodie, it's me."

"What happened? I heard gunfire."

The dog appeared at Miles' feet, jumping up and almost knocking him down. Miles patted the dog before shoving him away. "Too long to explain. We need to go. Where's Walker?"

Walker sat on a rock. Waved. His hands remained cuffed. "Present."

Miles got him up. Walker limped as they headed along a narrow trail that wound through a meadow of dead grass. Jodie hurried to catch up, but stumbled. Miles helped him. Between the darkness before them and his two companions, their pace was glacial. Even the dog appeared to sense it. He bounded forward a few steps and then looked back at them, ears up and eyes bright with moonlight.

When Miles caught Marshal Jodie as he struggled to climb across a deep furrow, Jodie threw his hand off him.

"I can manage fine, Kim. You have a compass in that metal brain?"

"Ruthie said take the east trail. We're heading east. I thought she would stay with you. The gang shot her and Dora down."

"Didn't even leave me a weapon. Not that it would do me much good. Eyes are funny since getting hit with that dart."

Miles handed him the spare pistol and reloaded his burner. He didn't imagine Gabriel's people would get horses up their trail, but it was what lay ahead that concerned him. The gang on horseback could find them and head them off and choose the ground for their next fight.

They'd lose moonlight soon. Already it was almost below the horizon, and a fresh patch of clouds threatened to take away their last light source at any moment.

"I can't..." Walker said. He leaned against a boulder, breathing hard.

Marshal Jodie pushed him along. "Get it in gear or get thumped."

"Wait," Miles said. "This spot's as good as the next. So far, none of us has twisted an ankle or broken anything. I'd rather not fall off a cliff. That would make it too easy for them."

"We'd be faster without him," Jodie said. "Heard they were looking for Walker, not us."

"I'm sure you're right. But he's our prisoner."

"Won't be if they take him from us after gunning us down."

The patch of rocks had enough places to sit or lean, but not get too comfortable. Jodie got Walker seated and eased himself down next to him. Miles settled in beside the dog, trying to find a spot where he had a view of the path ahead and behind. If anyone was coming for them, he'd see them. But as his breathing calmed and he had the luxury of contemplating the minor aches in his knees and back, he realized Insight was still pestering him.

Not an update. A facial recognition subroutine waited for his attention. A virtual pin stuck in the footage from the events of the evening.

He reviewed what Insight had waiting.

Gabriel's face looked straight at him and in profile. An old Meridian log sheet of known perps, something from the archives from his time as a cop. But the timestamp on the photo, along with the open warrant, was dated a decade before his service had begun with the Meridian military police. He hadn't even joined the army back then. It was the year before the Caretaker War had devolved into a full-blown conflict, and Gabriel already was wanted for terrorism, treasonous actions against Meridian Corporation, and murder.

Chapter Twenty-One

"Kim, you're mumbling to yourself," Marshal Jodie said.

Miles blinked hard to minimize Insight's display. Both Jodie and Walker were staring.

"I know him," Miles said.

"Know who? What are you talking about?"

"Gabriel the gang's leader. Insight just connected his face with a rap sheet. He was a wanted man in Meridian even before the war."

Jodie shook his head. "Something's wrong with your information, then. You've been retired for a while. If you're right, that would make Gabriel really old."

"Yeah. But he matches the sheet's face print and all the metrics perfectly. If the date's right, he's older than my dad."

"You saw him up close, didn't you? How old was he?"

"Not that old. I'd place him at fifty or sixty, tops."

"Then your Insight's wrong. You're exhausted. We're all tired and need a couple hours' sleep before we move. Shut it down and quit yapping."

Miles pulled up the rap sheet again, studied it, then scanned a zoomed-in still frame from the bar. No mistake. It was him. Gabriel Silva, real name unknown, several aliases, hyperlinks on Meridian's law enforcement net to known associates and organizations.

"It's not completely impossible that it's who you say, Marshal Kim," Paxton Walker offered.

Marshal Jodie hunkered into his coat. "Shut up. Keep it down, both of you."

Walker kept talking. "Genetic engineering has taken people towards the 180 mark. Rarified, to be sure, and mostly only for the Meridian faithful and top executive families, but not all. There are more radical efforts, many black market, that could account for him still being alive."

"But life extensions always show," Miles said. "Skin still gets worn out, the hair thins, the vocal cords weaken. The body pushes back in every way it can."

"Makeup and cosmetic surgery. Wigs, even. How closely did you see him?"

"I was close enough. And out here? I don't see any face renew clinics in the camp."

Walker chuckled. "Then he moisturizes and has a very good maintenance routine."

Jodie swatted Walker and raised a warning finger at Miles. "I said zip it, both of you. Not another word. We're too close to Manna. If they're scanning with audio sensors, they'll hear you."

Miles brought his hat down over his eyes. The dog was curled by his side and snoring. But sleep eluded Miles as he played the bar footage back. Gabriel in motion, talking, gesturing, dispensing justice.

The hyperlinks didn't work. Even if he were in River City, none of his files would synch with Meridian databases after his flight. The Insight module was stolen property. He was cut off. But Seraph net might have some of the information, if he could only get home.

And Seraph *was* home, wasn't it?

The thought the desert city was something more than a temporary last stop was firmly replaced with the notion it was where he would stay for a while. It's where Dillan and Zoe lived. And whatever his relationship with Santabutra Sin was becoming, he was actually looking forward to seeing her again. Missed her. The acerbic militia officer was growing on him, and he liked her hard humor and no-nonsense way. Never thought he'd bother starting a relationship again, and didn't know he had it in him.

Needed to get home first.

A place worth fighting for. That's why we do it.

His father's words, then his, at least what had come out of his mouth when he had joined Meridian service before understanding what any of the words really meant.

If Gabriel had been a young man answering the Caretaker call, had he likewise been naïve and innocent before committing what the rap sheet called "treasonous acts" and "murder"? If it was him, by some miracle of genetic enhancements, sensible diet, and makeup, what had he been doing in the southern wastes for so many years?

Jaya's words came to Miles. Gabriel and his gang had been at this for a long time. Never caught, because no one talked about it. Seraph was a new wrinkle in the desert, nothing more than a waystation and independent trading post before its growth during the past decade. Seraph justice was now intersecting with what had come before.

A rock kept digging into his back. Adjusting his position didn't help. He leaned, wiggled, and resolved they should move at the first hint of daylight. He blinked away the rap sheet and the footage.

Gabriel's identity provided context and a mystery, but it didn't color the fact that the gang needed to be stopped. He wanted to laugh at the thought that having two marshals was enough to make a difference with their situation.

Motion.

Insight dropped a target square. Miles cleared his burner from the holster. A squat, waddling animal the size of a horse's saddle ambled past, sniffing the air before hurrying off.

A badger, Insight said.

One more thing he didn't know enough about. It was the largest animal he had encountered in the wild. The others hadn't seen it, or at least hadn't stirred. His dog was watching, but Miles had ordered him to be quiet, and he obeyed.

"Jodie," Miles whispered.

Jodie grunted.

"How well can you describe this area?"

"Well enough. I know the camps. Time for a geography lesson when we make it back to Seraph."

"I don't want to wait that long. Tell me everything. I want to know what's where relative to our position. I'm guessing the gang will be out there waiting before we make it to anyplace that might have a signal."

"What are you thinking?"

"I'm thinking you help me make a mental map of where we are. And then we plot a course in the last direction they'd expect us to go."

Chapter Twenty-Two

The whirring of a drone began as a distant hum but grew louder with every passing moment.

Miles nudged Marshal Jodie, who tapped Walker with a heel of his boot. They all clustered around the largest rock, the dog wedging himself between Miles' feet.

"They'll see us," Jodie whispered.

Miles wiped crust from his left eye. "Depends on if that thing has infrared."

He listened, holding his breath. The flying machine was coming closer, but then the sound drifted away. His brain felt syrupy. His three-hour long stupor wasn't enough sleep. He hated having given in to it at all. Remembered many a third shift as a cop avoiding the trap of stims by taking a quick ten-minute power nap.

"Standing on my foot," Walker groaned.

Miles adjusted his position. The buzzing drone was still up there somewhere. Had the operator taken it higher for a better view? If they had night vision, it made sense. Then the whine grew louder. Insight tagged the drone with a target square.

Miles slid his burner out. "It's coming our way."

"You shoot it and they'll know we're here."

"They'll know anyway if it gets closer. Then they just have to keep it out of range and we won't be able to shake it."

Jodie sighed. "Take it out."

A single shot, then the drone plummeted. The engines kept whizzing until it crashed.

Miles put his weapon away. "No choice now. Let's get out of here."

Using his device, the screen light provided scant illumination across the ground ahead of them, but it was all they had. He strained his ears for the sign of another drone. The desert sky kept threatening rain, the stars obscured. Thunder sounded somewhere in the distance. No lightning. Now that the moon had set, the darkness was complete.

"They'll see the light," Jodie said.

Miles kept moving the beam on the trail at their feet and just far enough ahead so he wouldn't make a misstep. "We don't have a choice."

The dog kept to the trail ahead of them, sniffing back and forth before heading off out of sight. He returned minutes later, hackles up and staring intently at the path behind them.

Lights in the distance on their ridge, perhaps a kilometer back. Miles zoomed in. It was near where they had stopped. The rock formations caught some of the brilliant light beams as they played about. Their trail would be easily followed. If the gang was on foot, they might have a chance. On horseback?

"Keep going." Miles took Walker by the arm and moved him along.

Keeping his device's light close to the ground, he led them to the top of a switchback.

The dog barked. He stood a few meters back at the edge of some tall grass.

Jodie was about to descend. "What's the holdup?"

"Just a sec," Miles said. He went to the grass, but the dog wasn't waiting, bounding off through the vegetation instead. "Hey, dummy. Come back!"

"We don't have time for this. Kim!"

Miles tramped through some prickly thistles and directed his phone to where the dog was now waiting. A pair of rocks marked a track of sand. The dog whined, made a tentative step away, before again turning towards Miles.

He waved Jodie and Walker over. "This way."

"What are you talking about?" Jodie asked. "Here's the path off the ridge. They're coming. There's no time to cut a fresh path."

"They're probably going to catch us either way. Let's not make it easy for them."

The new trail ran down a gradual slope and soon had them navigating a narrow pass between walls of rock. Miles had no line of sight on their pursuers. The dog bounded ahead of them and waited, Miles doing his best to keep up while providing enough light for the others.

The sand gave way to a gulley that wound through an ever-deepening ravine. The compass said they were going south, the direction he wanted to go if they were to confound an ambush. Miles scanned the sky above in anticipation of a second drone. Nothing. The surrounding walls amplified distant thunder.

Walker eased himself over a large rock, his cuffed hands awkward in maintaining his balance. "Brilliant, sir marshal. Their mounts won't navigate the dicey terrain. But if we could stop and rest, even for a few minutes, I would be most grateful."

"Your voice carries," Miles said.

Walker was quiet for a while. When he fell a few minutes later, the clatter of cascading rocks echoed and made Miles wince. Walker shielded himself as Jodie yanked him to his feet.

"Let him sit," Miles said. "Ten minutes. Get your rest. Sky's getting lighter, and we're going to hit it hard once it does."

Jodie took Miles aside and spoke through a clenched jaw. "They're after him, not us. He's slow. It's a hard fact, Kim, but you're not stupid. We cut him loose and run. They find him, they leave us alone."

"You really think the gang will stop after they get him? I took out a few of them. I don't get the impression this Gabriel character is one to forgive and forget."

"He's going to get us caught."

"Keep an eye on Walker. I'm going to scout ahead."

Miles went up to where the dog waited. The ravine widened and split. The sky was a lighter blue, punctuated with the last of the stars visible between curtains of gray. Miles caught a whiff of ash or charcoal. A fire ring of stones lay next to a desiccated log that might have served as a hitching post. The dog sniffed at dried piles of horse dung. While it was too dark to look for tracks, either direction appeared to be easy walking.

He returned to Jodie and Walker and got them moving. Chose the left cut, which bore no marks of anyone having ridden in that direction.

As the clouds turned pink, they marched between low hills and yellow weeds. A surprised rabbit rocketed from a bramble directly in front of the dog. The dog chased it and ran out of sight, only to return minutes later with nothing to show for his effort.

They were heading south. Twenty minutes after sunset, they intercepted a trail with fresh signs of horses and wheeled vehicles having passed that way. Miles climbed to the top of a rise to get a better view. No one in sight, but the hills might conceal any number of gang members following them. How long would it take the gang to realize they weren't going towards any of the closest camps?

"Anything?" Jodie called.

Miles shook his head. Then something caught his eye. On a plateau several kilometers south was another tower, thin and almost invisible in the haze. He scanned the ground between him and the tower, marking the location. Marshal Jodie whistled for his attention. Waved him over. They had found an overflowing water trough fed by a trickling pipe at the base of a rock wall. The rock face bled seeping rivulets of rust. The dog snuffled around the trough before lapping at some of the runoff.

They drank.

"No camps marked south of here?" Miles asked.

Jodie wiped his bristly mouth. Spat. "You're the one with the map in his head. It's like I told you. We don't go this far south. There's nothing down here. We're off the range, and I don't like it."

"You must have heard something. This spring and that tower says someone lives here."

"Yeah? And what makes you think they'll be happy to see us?"

Miles ignored the comment and checked on Walker's feet. Blisters, blood, and weeping sores. His hobble would only get worse, but eventually he wouldn't be able to continue, even if they could somehow replace his shoes.

While Walker rested, Miles played with the captured radio, moving through each of the twenty preset channels. There hadn't been a chance to use it while on the move. He went through each twice, hearing dead air, until he made out a hiss, pop, and the fraction of a word before silence. He clipped the radio to his belt with the volume up. The range on the handset might be a couple of kilometers under ideal circumstances.

"They're not far."

Jodie shuffled closer. "This is a prime stopping location. A pinch point, if they're looking for us down here. Can't assume they don't know about it."

Miles got under one of Walker's arms as the man faltered. "Let's find a place to lie low."

Chapter Twenty-Three

The rusting metal windmill leaned precariously over the shattered remains of an adobe cottage. The steel of the windmill was pockmarked and had a dangling chain that appeared to have once been connected to the remains of a small motor.

A wall of the cottage stood tall enough to provide shade. Walker made a beeline for it.

Jodie stopped him. "Wait." He checked the sections of wall and the brush.

"What is it?" Walker asked.

"Snakes, mostly. And scorpions. Have a seat."

Walker chose a section of clear ground and squatted, not wanting anything to do with the shade. Miles monitored the trail below them. While the windmill was a landmark, there were enough rocks nearby they could properly hide if he spotted anyone. There were other run-down ruins, all of them overgrown with vines and grass.

He wished he had drunk more water. With no canteen, they couldn't go much further in the growing heat of the morning, Walker's feet notwithstanding.

The dog dutifully scrutinized a collapsed corner of the house before relieving himself. Walker grimaced in disgust. Miles hoped it meant he wouldn't have to figure out how to empty the robot's insides. As the dog finished his business and joined Miles, he felt a certain jealousy and wondered at what point could his parts be replaced one at a time before he became so carefree.

Humans. Animals. Machines. The rabbit, the badger, the dog, him, Gabriel the Judge—lines of code, that's all they were. No matter how you slice it.

Dust in the spring's direction. Miles got Jodie's attention and collected Walker, assisting him to the cover of the rocks where they got down in the dirt. The dog found a place near Jodie, who had no problem keeping low.

"What about the snakes?" Walker whispered.

Miles pushed his head down. "Don't let them smell your fear and you'll be fine."

Walker rolled his eyes.

Three riders walking their horses appeared on the road. Not the source of the dust. The lead man looked like one of the gang members from the bar. He raised a pair of binoculars and surveyed their hillside.

Miles didn't move. He was in the shade, peeking, with no chance of sunlight reflecting off anything.

The buzz of a small engine rose steadily. A quad bike caught up to the riders, the tires kicking up a plume. The leather-clad driver exchanged a few words and hand signals with the three before zipping off ahead of them, the riders continuing at their slower pace.

"Can you get 'em?" Jodie hissed.

"No. Stay down."

"How many?"

"Four. At least for now."

They were just outside of what Miles considered a sure shot. The last thing he wanted was to get pinned down. And if the binoculars had any additional sensors, they might pick up his targeting. A few minutes later, the riders were gone.

Miles got up and endured a moment while both knees let their discomfort be known. "We're clear."

Jodie shielded his eyes and searched the road in both directions. "Well, that's just great. Now they're in front of us and behind. You should have taken the shot."

"They might guess we came this way, but they can't know for sure.

Right now they're split up. Sniping at them will only bring the whole gang down on us."

Walker sat on a rock and began picking grit from his slippers. "How much further?"

"This spot's as good as any. Stay here for the heat of the day until evening. Then we keep going towards that antenna and see if there's a camp nearby."

Marshal Jodie muttered something under his breath. He climbed to the top of a boulder and stared at the trail, occasionally rubbing his eyes. The dog found a spot of sand and lay down.

"Stay put. I'll be back." Miles climbed up the hill. It was a risk if there were more spotters searching for them, but it was a big desert, and he tried his best to move slowly and keep down when possible. Near the crest, he found a commanding view of the land southeast of them. The arid stretch of earth vanished into a rising shimmer of heat. He couldn't see or hear anyone.

The parched ground provided a hardscrabble existence to a dozen types of weeds. Besides rabbits and badgers, there had to be other creatures living in the harsh climate. The ruins below were a stark reminder not everyone made it.

When something chimed, he reached for the handset radio first before realizing he had an incoming call. He almost dropped the phone as he took it out. The damaged screen lit up but was devoid of any data.

He tapped it to answer. "This is Miles. I copy. Are you there?"

The last voice he expected was his son, Dillan.

"Dad, where are you?"

He held the phone as if looking at it wrong might break it. "Dillan? Hello, Dillan? Can you hear me?"

Silence. He didn't dare touch the screen nor shift from his position. Had the phone muted? Or had the call been his imagination?

"I'm listening," he said. "I'm pretty far out of Seraph network range. If you're getting this, I need help. Dillan, I need to you call Marshal Barma. We're..." A quick consultation with Insight and a little math on how far they had traveled gave him the information he needed. "...thirty-six kilometers south-southeast of Seraph, and about nine kilometers south of a camp called Manna. We need help and backup. Tell me you got that."

"Dad, I hear you, but I can't understand…" Fuzz cut off his son. Miles waited a moment. "…say something about help?"

Miles tried to keep his voice calm. Repeated his instructions. "Confirm you got that. You need to call Marshal Barma. You got that? I'll repeat: we're thirty-six—"

The dual-tone beep told him the call had disconnected.

Chapter Twenty-Four

Miles waited for five unbearable minutes for the phone to ring again before tapping the screen, lighting it up, and letting muscle memory guide his fingers to enable voice command.

"Call Marshal Barma."

The no signal chime forced a sigh from him as he tried again. "Call Marshal Barma." "Call Seraph net emergency line." "Call Dillan Kim."

The polite tone kept repeating. He gripped the device tighter and tighter and forced himself to unclench his hand. He held it aloft, as if an arm's length might change things. It didn't. After a few more tries, he put the phone away.

He was sweating by the time he made it back to Jodie and Walker at the collapsed hut. The clouds from the weather front were broken into a fan of streams and puffballs. Whatever rain had fallen had already evaporated, lending the air a balminess not entirely unpleasant.

Miles found a spot in the shade near Walker.

Jodie was staring at him. "Sun's going to be overhead soon. We don't have shelter."

"I got a hint of a signal. Might improve if I get closer to that tower."

"That'll put you out in the open. Do I need to remind you they have snipers? And there's no way to know if there's anything up there worth the bother."

"The track here leads somewhere. And someone put that tower up. The gang went this way, so there might be something they think would bring us south."

"Or they're following in our footsteps and it's a matter of time before they realize they've lost us and circle back. You shouldn't have climbed the hill."

Miles ignored the comment. "We wait a few hours and go back to the spring. We drink up. We come back here, then you two hide and I'll try for the antenna and see if I can get there by sundown."

Jodie didn't comment. It was stay, turn back north, keep going on the track, or cut a fresh path into the wastes. None of the choices were optimal.

The dog was staring.

"Don't suppose you understand enough to go get us help," Miles said. "Emergency mode? A signal booster in that head of yours?"

The robot animal's unconcerned expression vanished as he took notice of a circling buzzard. The bird did a few lazy turns overhead before moving on. Then the dog went to sleep.

Miles resolved to get a user manual for his pet.

Miles took point when they headed back towards the water trough. It was past two in the afternoon, with extra levels of heat beating down on them as they made it to the trail. Walker's feet had swollen, and his pace was slower than ever. Jodie assisted him. The marshal hadn't said a word since reprimanding Miles for his trek up the hill.

Making the water trough was one thing. Once they got a drink, would they be able to get Walker back to their hiding place? But getting dehydrated or suffering heat stroke would do the gang's work for them. Surviving long enough to get their fugitive home meant they had to live through the day. Walker hadn't spoken much either. His eyes were sunken and his lips were cracked. But thirst proved a powerful motivator.

The trough was as they had first found it, with no one in view. Miles made it there first. He washed his face and slicked his hair back before dipping his hat in the water and placing it on his head. The others collapsed next to the trough and drank. The dog circled about, examining the fresh tire and horse tracks.

A thought came to Miles. He motioned for the dog. "Come here, boy. Drink."

The dog began lapping up water. After a moment, he looked at Miles expectantly.

"More. As much as you can swallow. And no peeing."

"What are you doing, Kim?" Marshal Jodie asked.

"Your fellow marshal has lost his mind," Walker said.

Miles stroked the dog's head. "The dog isn't real. It's a bot I found, and I never located its owner. It doesn't need water. But we do. And I figure it can hold a gallon or so, maybe more."

Walker frowned. "How do you get the water out?"

"Haven't figured it out yet."

"You've had a robot dog all this time and kept it from us?" Jodie asked incredulously. "Send it for help."

"Far as I can tell, it doesn't have a message system."

"You want to use the thing as a walking canteen, but you can't get it to run to the nearest camp?"

"I tried to get it to do just that. It won't or can't. I haven't had time to learn what it's capable of. So unless you have paper and pencil or some way of attaching a message, that won't work. And I've run into enough scrappers to know they might take this thing and sell its parts once they figure out what it is. Drink up. We stick to the plan."

Whatever comprehension was going on in the robot canine's brain remained hidden by a chummy grin as the dog panted with his tongue out.

"Hello, marshals," Gabriel's voice said from the hand radio.

Miles took it from his belt and turned it up. Jodie was shaking his head and mouthing "do not answer." Miles raised a hand and nodded.

"Marshals, in case you are listening to this, know that we are intent on bringing the man in your custody to justice. There doesn't have to be any more violence. I will allow you to return to Seraph unharmed. Reply to this and let me know where you've left him, and you will be free to return home. I will listen for your reply on channel three."

Walker rose shakily to his feet. "They're coming. We have to hide."

Miles got up and looked around. He caught Walker before he fell. "Take it easy. They're fishing."

"They're close. Those radios have a short range. They know where we are."

"He's not wrong," Marshal Jodie said. "They're near, and this watering hole is a trap. Give me the radio, Kim. While we have time."

"What are you talking about?" Miles asked. "We hide. We wait it out up in the rocks and get to the antenna."

"Walker can't go any further. And you said it yourself, we can't fight them. So hand me the radio or call him yourself. We get out of here alive and come back when we have backup."

Walker was shaking his head. "Marshal Kim, you're not seriously—"

"Zip it, Paxton," Miles said. "I'm not giving our prisoner over to them. You can't believe a word Gabriel's saying. After what I saw, you'd know what he's capable of."

"They shot me with that dart by accident. They would have finished the job if they meant to. This Gabriel thinks this is his territory, so we yield ground. Doesn't mean we're giving up. But I'm not dying with Walker when we can both leave him behind and survive to fight another day."

"I told you what I'm doing. You hide, I get the word out. We don't abandon our prisoner."

"Broke phone, a dog full of piss, and your burner? It's no good. I'm senior marshal. I'm giving you an order."

"And I'm saying no."

When Marshal Jodie went for the pistol on his belt, Miles had his burner up a split second faster.

"Don't," Miles said.

But Jodie wasn't stopping, finger on the trigger, and bringing his weapon clear of the fabric of his shirt. Miles fired. Jodie's weapon discharged. A clap of thunder exploded, and a bullet punched the dirt at Miles' feet. Jodie howled and clutched his chest before pitching backwards into the dirt.

"You shot...you shot..." Jodie gasped. His hands clutched the wound, trembled, and finally let out a sigh and stopped moving.

Miles' heart raced and he realized he was holding his breath as he nudged the pistol away from Jodie.

"I saw it," Walker said. "I saw it all. He was trying to shoot you. He was going to kill you because of me."

"Be quiet."

Miles crouched next to Jodie and found no pulse. The neat burn mark over his heart and the blank stare told him everything. He patted Jodie down. Took the badge and picked up the pistol from the dirt.

"What are we going to do?" Walker asked.

"Gun shots made enough noise they will have heard. Change of plan."

He yanked Jodie's boots off and handed them to Walker. Best estimate? They'd fit.

Walker's lips curled. "That's indecent."

"I can't argue with that. But you need them more than he does. Put them on."

As Walker removed the remains of his tattered jail slippers off and pulled on the marshal's boots, Miles made a final assessment of Jodie's body and decided there was nothing to be done except leave him where he lay.

Walker winced as he wriggled his feet. "They're tight."

"Beats what you had. If you can't continue, they'll catch you. Get up. We're going to start walking, and we're not stopping until we make it to that tower."

Chapter Twenty-Five

"Marshal Kim, what have you done?" Gabriel again on the radio, now with a bemused tone. "Did you hear my plea? Did your prisoner get the best of you and kill you and Marshal Jodie? Or did something else drive a wedge between you, forcing your hand?"

Miles shuffled a step behind Walker, who trudged along with his arms dangling and head bobbing. The stretch of hardpan might have only been several kilometers, but it felt like fifty. The sun seemed to have drawn closer, compressing the sky and drawing the oxygen from the air.

Even the dog slogged along. Miles wondered if the bot's dying in the desert performance was a subroutine based on observed animal behavior.

What Miles had guessed would be a two-hour hike to the hill and up to the antenna was now three. Walker kept moving, but his pace was a crawl as they began the ascent up a gradual incline.

"The ground tells a tale, marshal," Gabriel continued over the handset. "You still live, as does Paxton Walker. You're close. It's a matter of time before we find you both. The desert doesn't suffer fools and will claim you. We both seek justice as our vocation. And while the law has nuance and enforcement has room for subtleties, a proven transgressor must face his crimes, for the good of the land, the community, and their soul."

Walker had stopped. Wiped his brow and blinked as if having trouble seeing. "Turn it off."

"Keep going," Miles said.

Gabriel's voice was crystal clear. Was his sharpshooter even now sighting them through a scope? Miles hoped the rising heat might obscure them. Focused on his next step and finishing their climb. Thoughts of Marshal Jodie's last moments kept replaying. A fraction of a second faster, he might have targeted a hand or Jodie's weapon. A better read of Jodie's body language, and Miles could have wrestled the gun away.

The simmer in his intestines made him want to retch.

No matter how he approached it, giving Walker over hadn't been and still wasn't an option. But he couldn't shake the niggling in his brain that somehow a compromise might have been reached and Jodie would still be alive.

The hill grew steeper, with broken ground ahead. They had departed from the trail, opting to take a direct route that had given them some cover in a shallow wadi. But now they would be exposed as they intersected the path again and were walking where horses and vehicles had passed recently.

The antenna towering above them was twice as high as the ones used by Manna and the camps to the north. A dish was fixed to one side, along with several smaller aerials. A power station with solar panels was hooked up and hummed with life. Power. It had power. Miles took out his phone, wiped sweat from his eyes, and turned the phone on. The screen wouldn't light. He tried again, rubbing his damp left hand on his pants before tapping the cracked screen, then the power button, but the device refused to do anything.

"You can call for help now, right?" Walker asked.

Miles stared at his useless device. "No, I can't."

"Maybe someone down there can help."

A row of adobe huts lined one wall of a gulch to the southwest. Miles moved past the antenna for a better look. Trees grew in the shadows near a row of massive white plastic water tanks. Around them stood more structures of mud or clay.

Miles scanned for signs of life. Another ghost town, he thought, but then a dog appeared from one hut, followed by a toddler. A garden grew next to the home.

Walker began shuffling. "There's people there. We get help. We'll be safe."

"Hold on. There's people, all right, but what people? You know this place?"

"No."

"This could be where the gang lives. Or they come here enough that they're allied with Gabriel. We don't know. Marshal Jodie didn't even mention this camp. We can't assume they're friendly."

Walker's voice cracked. "Then what do we do, Marshal Kim? Die?"

"We watch and wait. Follow me."

What had looked like a flat stretch of rock turned out to be the buried top level of an old parking garage. The second level was half-filled with dirt, but there was plenty of shade that proved to be an instant relief from the afternoon sun.

Walker took the first spot clear of debris he could find and flopped down. Miles made a quick examination of their shelter before bringing the dog over. The drain spigot was under a flap of fur near the robot's stomach. At least the designer had some sense of decorum, as if expecting the need for someone in Miles' situation or at least affording dignity to the robot's wealthy owners, who would need to perform the maintenance task of draining their expensive toy.

Water dribbled out, and Miles put his mouth to the drain and drank. When Walker saw what he was doing, he crawled over, his dry lips moving in anticipation. Miles gave Walker his turn at the dog. The bot stood solemnly by, as if the procedure was nothing but a minor inconvenience. The water tasted warm to hot and carried the cutting aroma of solvent. Once they both had their fill, Miles closed the spigot.

"That...tasted awful," Walker said.

He had his new boots off and was examining his swollen feet. Miles took the boots as he ducked back out of their shelter.

"Where are you going?" Walker asked.

"I'm taking a look around. See if anyone has a ride or a horse we can steal or buy."

"But...my footwear."

"Yeah." Miles held up the boots. "Without these, I know you'll stay put." He made a kissing sound. The dog bounded over and followed close at his heels.

At a cracked concrete abutment, he found a spot with shade where he could watch both the antenna and the gulch. Thick brambles obscured the slope just below him. A stone shelf jutted from the hill further down. The top of a collapsed building or overpass? What caught his eye was a splash of color and a sparkling reflection of sunlight. Mirrors, he thought, but then realized it was a collection of bottles.

"Wait here," he told the dog.

A quick slide through thorny weeds led him to the top of what had once been a roadway but was now a bare lot infested with tumbleweeds. Seven blankets were laid out, each replete with fruit, ears of corn, nuts, vegetables, and knick-knacks, including the bottles. It was another market, like the one Jaya had explained to him at the signal station.

Three crude tarp canopies stood at one end. A person sat hunkered beneath each shelter, bundled as if it were a chilly day and not a sweltering blast furnace in hell. Three women, he decided, old, and appearing indifferent to his appearance as he looked at them and again at the proffered wares.

"Do any of you have a radio?" When none of the three answered, he took his badge off his hip and showed it to them. "I'm Marshal Kim with Seraph. We've had trouble. I need to borrow a radio."

One woman in a black leather vest leaned towards another. The quick words were impossible to follow, and Insight had no joy in translating them. A Native American language?

"Look, this is an emergency. Can you understand me? Someone in your camp has a radio. I see the tower. If you can tell me who I should ask, that would be helpful."

The middle woman had a receding hairline, but a long gray fan of hair draped on her shoulders. A headband with bright beadwork was on her head.

She pointed a knobby forefinger at the blankets. "Trade."

"You want something for the information?" Miles asked.

She muttered a few words and one of the others grunted as if agreeing.

Miles didn't want to give up the pair of boots in his hand. Standing out in the open left him feeling exposed. But the women had seen him, and he needed to play his hand.

He took Marshal Jodie's pistol from his belt. After removing the bullets from the magazine, he placed the weapon on the blanket. "That's what I have to offer. Here's what I want in exchange. Access to a radio. Even better, to borrow a horse or motorbike. Can one of you give me a ride north? You give me a ride, you get the gun. Deal?"

The middle woman stared at the gun, then at him with steely eyes. It took her a moment to get up. She leaned over the blanket, pointing to a gourd and a bushel basket of prickly pears. The thought of juice and some fruit was heady, and Miles didn't want to think about how hungry he was.

"No," he said. "A ride. A horse, car, motorbike. Only to borrow. You keep the gun."

She hadn't touched the weapon, but kept looking at it before considering her own assortment of wares. She pointed to more: a handmade obsidian cutting knife with a twine handle. A plate of flatbreads. A bowl of dried peppers. She made a circle of all of it, then pointed at the pistol.

He shook his head. "Still not good enough."

She coughed, obviously disappointed. Looked at the other two women in the sun shelters. The one in the black vest waved her off, the other shook her head. So much for collective bargaining.

She *tsk-tsk-tsked*, muttered something to herself, and shuffled off down a slope towards a row of huts.

End of negotiations.

He was about to pick up the pistol when the woman in the black vest waved at him. Words and sign language followed. Miles could decipher enough of it to know she wanted him to leave the weapon where it lay.

So he waited.

The woman with the gray hair returned ten minutes later pushing a bicycle. She rolled it to him and stared. What had once been a yellow frame was now mostly bare steel. The gears, pedals, and chain appeared clean. Thin tires, but the wheel rims were solid and free of corrosion.

"A ride," she said in a thick voice. "For the gun."

Five minutes later he had the bike, a gourd, and a half bag of prickly pears. The women were laughing as he struggled to get the bike up the hill, dropping nothing. It wasn't until he got to the top that he spotted a rough set of earthen steps near the edge of the parking garage.

Both embarrassed and exhausted, he turned back to look down at the traders to wave. That was when he saw the woman in the black vest talking on a device and gesturing in his direction.

Chapter Twenty-Six

At least they had a bicycle.

The problem was the gang *knew* they had a bike, thanks to the woman at the market. They also had their location and would find them if Miles and Walker didn't keep moving. The small seat barely accommodated a single rider with a fanny the size of a pair of plums, but somehow Miles peddled standing while his prisoner occupied the seat while hanging on for dear life.

The steady keen of an electric motorcycle gave them enough time to hit the dirt. They landed hard. The sound came from somewhere directly above them.

They had been riding for only moments, having sped downhill from the parking garage on the side of the plateau away from the village. The sun was low, leaving them plenty of shadow. But the prospects for a good hiding place were slim.

Miles kept Walker's head down. As the dust settled, the dog perked up and barked.

"No!" Miles hissed. "Bad dog!"

The dog was quiet for the moment, his attention fixed on the crest of the plateau. The engine sound cut out. Someone was up there searching, and all they had to do was look down. As they waited, Miles stifled a cough. The bag of prickly pears lay smushed beneath him, and the gourd, with what had turned out to be fermented juice, was leaking.

"Can you shoot him?" Walker asked.

"Shhh."

"Steal his bike? I can call out and feign surrender."

"Be quiet, or I shoot you myself."

While Walker's suggestion wasn't terrible and the idea of an upgrade to a motorbike enticing, there was no way to know who was above them. Was it even a gang member or someone from the village? If the latter, then would he be justified in ending their life for trying to aid in their capture?

Miles felt a sense of relief when the motorbike's engine started up again and the bike drove off. He got their bicycle up and collected what they had dropped. The gourd continued to dribble out its contents. He took a swig before passing it to Walker.

"Not much left," Miles said. "Finish up."

The track they were on barely made up a trail and was little more than a cut in the ground running downhill at a steep angle. At least it was free of rocks and navigable. If the sun was going to set, he wanted to find some place where they had good visibility and cover.

A grove of junipers was hardly sufficient, but it was large enough and grew across a deep rut, little more than a dirt ditch. It would suffice as a hiding hole for the moment. After sliding down, he parked the bike and made a quick survey. No signs anyone used the spot as a campground, and no footprints or tire marks in the dirt.

He checked his device for good measure. Screen still dark. They would have to use what light they had to get comfortable.

Walker opened the bag of prickly pear. "It's suffered calamity, I'm afraid."

"Eat what you can. Watch out for the needles."

They took turns with the crushed fruit, scooping sweet, sticky goop with their fingers. It did little to ease the hunger. He checked the dog, but there was no way to be sure how much water it still carried.

Walker wiped his fingers on a rock. "Washing down our repast would be nice."

"We'll want to save every drop for tomorrow."

"That's the plan? This is hardly safe here. Perhaps if we slink back into camp, we might find food and a better means of transport."

"The bike's a minor miracle. Going back is too big a risk. The entire gang might come down here, and if the moon's out, I'm thinking we try to ride north."

Walker looked like he was going to say more, but only nodded.

Miles propped the bike up so it would be in place in case they needed to bug out. The dog remained antsy, sitting, moving, following, and whining. Normal behavior, or was the robot animal keying in on his own apprehension?

When Miles sat, the dog settled in next to him. Miles was afraid to relax, didn't want to slip into a slumber. Despite the nagging doubts about every step that led him to where he was, his body craved rest.

He wanted to curse Jodie. Gabriel and his outlaws, too. Damn all of them for placing him here, with a two-bit con man who had chosen Miles' first day on the job to make his escape. Miles could have been content with his security gig, working easy nights with Tristan. Found satisfaction helping at the Church of the Sands kitchen or any other charities that might use an extra set of hands, be they flesh or metal.

So why accept Barma's invitation? Pride? Self-identity? Making a difference?

The cliché probably went back to the first professional soldier or cop to don a uniform. Even the murkiest of security forces and every armed bully must have believed the world would be better with them than without. Without meant anarchy. But here, outside of the range of Seraph law, the camps functioned, even if it meant submitting to a psychopath and his minions' flavor of justice.

He eyed Walker. "Why you?"

"Marshal?"

"Gabriel wants you, not me. So what is it? He doesn't care that you escaped from a Seraph lockup. What has him so motivated?"

Boots off again, Walker had his knees drawn to his chest as he inspected angry blisters on his toes. "Perhaps my associate besmirched my name. Bad company corrupts poor character, right marshal?"

"I don't buy that. Unless his running into Foxglove was a coincidence, Gabriel found him at the spring. He took the time to destroy his radio and camp and didn't bother dragging him back to Manna for any trial. Same with Ruthie's man Ivan. That one smells like an ambush."

"I didn't know Ivan."

"But you knew Foxglove."

"He was my ticket to New Pacific. That's it. I radioed him from the prison a few days before I could slip away. Perhaps this Gabriel has me confused with someone else."

"Hmm."

As the sky grew darker, Miles tried to ignore Walker's constant groaning. It was only as he faded to sleep did he dimly realize Walker had stopped fussing. It was the sound of the bike wheels that woke him. A shadow—Walker's—had the bike in hand and was running with it, shoving it up the embankment.

Miles scrambled to get up. The dog was barking and at his side as he clambered after Walker. His prisoner had made the top of their ditch but was having trouble getting his boots on the pedals. He got rolling forward when Miles tackled him. They went down with a clatter.

Walker let out a resounding "Oof!" Squirmed. Miles punched him across the face. A second blow to his stomach, and Walker moaned and lay still. Miles remained on top of him, his arm poised to strike a third time. Walker pawed at him. "I yield. Stop!"

A white beam cut through the dark and swept the surrounding desert. It bobbed up and down momentarily before settling on a patch of boulders a hundred meters away. More lights joined the first, an array of bright floods and headlights. A desert runner was bouncing over the hard ground and racing in their direction, a spotlight and light rack turning night into day.

Miles kept low and hauled Walker across the dirt and back down into their ditch. The dog was with them, but the bicycle wasn't. The vehicle's engine roared as it got closer. If they had good eyes, they'd see the bike. If they had a software suite with sensors, the vehicle operators would have them cold.

Tires crunched on rocks. Twigs and brush snapped as the runner slowed and drove through the brambles. But the lights were shining away now. The engine revved and the tires spun, then the runner was driving off.

Walker had stopped struggling. Miles got off him and peered over the edge of the furrow.

The searchlight continued to scan the night as the vehicle headed west, vanishing and reappearing as it navigated the rough ground.

Miles climbed out of the hiding place and retrieved the bike. He surveyed the desert. The distant runner was making a turn and heading off in a new direction. But a second car was out there too, also with lights, and they appeared to be making a circuit around the plateau.

"They know we're here," Miles said as he joined Walker.

Walker was pressing a hand to his mouth. "Did they see us?"

"No. Guessing they don't have an AI or advanced audio. Otherwise they would have heard you." Miles leaned the bike against a dirt wall. "If you would have run, they would have caught you. I'm guessing if they catch you, I get to go home."

"Which you won't do, marshal. It's why you shot Marshal Jodie."

"Yeah."

Miles remained standing and leaning on the lip of the trench, studying the moving shapes patrolling the darkness. Walker had settled down again. Miles considered again confiscating his prisoner's boots, but decided against it. If they had to change locations in a hurry, he wanted nothing slowing them down. He set Insight to chime an alarm every fifteen minutes to help him stay alert.

They wouldn't be riding away from their hiding place soon. Instead, this patch of sunken earth might be their last stand.

Chapter Twenty-Seven

Near dawn, and he was flagging. Insight kept waking him as instructed, and he was turning off the alarm by rote.

The desert runners were out there somewhere, their engines loud enough to carry across the dry expanse. But they had ranged further and further until, for the past two hours, Miles couldn't see their lights or hear them.

"Do you really think we can make it?" Walker asked. The man's voice was hoarse, and it might have been the second time he asked.

"It's too light out. This spot's as good as any. We stay put."

"For another day here?"

Miles glanced at him. "You can leave if you'd like. But the bike's mine."

Walker sat back sulkily. Eyed the dog. "I'm thirsty."

They drank what was left inside the dog, but it wasn't much, about a mouthful for each. The dog eyed Miles warily, as if worrying Miles would shake him down for the last drops in his reservoir. Their hiding spot wouldn't be out of the sun once the day began. The juniper bushes would make for poor shade. The sun began cresting over the distant eastern hills.

An engine hummed in the distance. Too throaty a rumble for a motorcycle. Miles took his hat off and kicked out a dirt step in the embankment so he could get a look.

It was a militia buggy. The six-wheel vehicle cruised along the caliche in a straight line that would take it towards the plateau. With his right eye, he zoomed in. Red Banner insignia on the door. The vehicle might have a lone driver, it might have a squad of six troopers. Either way, unless the gang had captured the buggy, it was from Seraph, and he had to make contact.

He grabbed the bike. "Stay here."

"Where are you going?"

"That's a Red Banner cruiser. Either it's a long-range patrol or they're looking for us. Keep out of sight. I don't want to take your boots."

Miles didn't wait for Walker to protest. He flung the bike from the trench and climbed out, picking the bike up again, straddling it, and launching himself forward. A wave of dizziness struck him, but he started pedaling, weaving around the rocks and broken ground. He wanted to shout and wave, but decided it would be best to intercept the militia buggy before they missed him entirely.

He coasted down a wide furrow and pedaled hard as he came up the opposite side. The buggy wasn't slowing down or changing course. If he didn't hurry, they'd be out of sight past a cluster of boulders.

"Come on, come on," he chided himself. His legs burned. The early sun fell hot on his face, and he realized he didn't have his hat. As he ascended a small rise, he was in the best spot to be seen, yet the buggy continued headlong.

"Open your eyes, you idiots!"

The buggy was almost at the boulders. Then Miles saw something which twisted his guts into a knot. A half-dozen figures were keeping cover around the largest of the rocks. They were holding weapons.

Miles stopped the bike, waved, shouted. The buggy was a klick and a half away. He drew his burner. Sighted at the figures.

No target, Insight said.

Out of range. He fired anyway. Couldn't see if he hit anything, but two of the figures were pointing his direction now. One of them shouldered a rifle. He saw the muzzle flash before the bullet missed him, followed by the *ka-KRAK* of the report. He flinched but didn't move. A gang member was now on top of the largest boulder. He hoisted a tube to his shoulder. But he wasn't aiming at Miles.

The *whoosh* and trail of propellant that darted for the buggy were almost instantaneous, but for Miles, it felt like it happened in slow motion. The rocket struck the militia car head on and exploded in a thunderclap of dark gray dust, followed by the palpable slap of a shockwave that braced Miles' face.

The ambushers were likewise stunned by the explosion, but the momentary inertia passed quickly. The man on top of the boulder scrambled down. One of them had a horse by the reins. Surely they'd have more horses and vehicles. The shooter with the rifle raised their weapon.

Miles turned and fled, working the pedals as hard as he could.

Had they known the Red Banners were coming? Must have, to have that kind of firepower prepped. Gabriel's gang had communications, armaments, motor vehicles, and they'd bring all of them down on Miles if he didn't move.

Walker was scrambling out of their ditch. "What was that explosion?"

"Gabriel and his gang. Climb on."

"Where?" was all Walker could manage before he once again perched on the back half of the miniscule seat and clamped onto Miles.

The south side of the plateau was a broken wash of craggy ground with little vegetation and no rock formations. Too late to turn back, Miles realized. He cut across a series of ruts along a road leading to points south and headed out into the featureless desert ahead of them. Faraway hills and mesas lay to all sides, but the distances were hard to guess without stopping.

The only advantage they had was a head start, and that would vanish once a spotter saw which way they were heading.

He almost crashed as the ground dropped away into a wide channel running roughly north and south. North would bring them closer to the plateau. It wouldn't be deep enough to conceal them. So once again, he chose south and pedaled.

They fell three times in two hours until Miles could no longer keep the bicycle moving. He pushed the bike along, the dog taking lead, although the bot made a show of appearing sluggish.

Walker kept a hand on the bike's seat as he hobbled next to it, frequently stopping to adjust his boots. "We lost them, didn't we?"

"Probably." Miles hated to waste his strength on pointless speculation. Gabriel and his minions had proven themselves more than a roving troupe setting up court in the scattered camps at the fringes of Seraph. This was their domain, and he was being forced deeper into their territory. And if they had evaded the gang, the desert would have its say.

The Red Banners wouldn't let losing a squad go unanswered, but if the buggy had been out of communication range, it might be written off as lost. If more patrols came, it would be too late for them to help Miles.

His mouth and throat were devoid of moisture. He was tempted to try the dog again for any last precious drops, but feared if he stopped now, he wouldn't recover.

What if Jodie was right?

He hated the thought. Perhaps the gang might have killed them all like they had executed the Alcotts. But if either he or Jodie had made it out, the militia squad could have been warned.

The wadi leveled out and left them trudging on hard soil. Two hills lay ahead, with no sign of anyone having passed this way. But the trail they had crossed ran roughly in this direction. With no hint of cover, he directed them between the hills. That was when motion caught his eye up ahead.

Something flapped in the air, the almost imperceptible breeze catching what appeared at first to be a banner or flag. A sail on a boat, he thought irrationally, a vessel come to take them from the wastes to some elsewhere island paradise.

He blinked and focused. Not a sail, not flags, but vapor collectors. There was nowhere to hide, so he directed the bike and Walker towards them. The large polymer sheets made a soft fluttering sound. A water tank sat beneath them. A power source hummed from a transformer box nestled beneath the collectors.

He leaned the bicycle against the base of a collector array and circled the tank. A pipe ran off it between the hills where several domed shelters had been set up. Solar panels wrapped around each dome. From the camp came the bleating of goats.

The tank had a spigot near the pipe. Miles opened it and drank, almost choking as the water hit his parched throat. He motioned for Walker to likewise drink, but his prisoner needed no invitation and greedily sucked down water and splashed more across his face.

He checked the charge on his burner. Pointed at the camp, at himself, and made a walking motion with his fingers.

Walker's sunburned expression was hard to read. Miles left him, the dog, and the bike behind as he stalked along the pipe towards the camp, trying to clear his head and strain his ears. If Walker had some hidden reservoir of strength and was going to nab the bike and run for it, Miles couldn't stop him.

The camp was larger than it looked, with twenty or more of the shelters. Palm trees grew between the domes. A dozen elderly people reclined on lounge chairs in the shade, with a few more sitting slumped in wheelchairs. One gray-haired woman in a thin patchwork frock was pacing back and forth, her frail arms curled and her jaw jittery.

A middle-aged woman appeared with a tray. Straight black hair below the ears, long yellow buttoned dress to her ankles, she moved between the residents as she distributed tiny paper cups. Some drank, others stared at her confused. She crouched beside one man in a wheelchair. "Drink your juice, Philip. You need your vitamins. But drink slow. I don't want you coughing again."

Miles remained crouched behind the corner of a small greenhouse walled with plastic sheeting. As he zoomed in to watch, he realized the woman looked familiar. If not for the shorter hair, she was a spitting image of Jaya. She vanished for a moment, only to return, this time handing out cookies.

The thought of juice, food, and assistance sent a wave of lightheadedness through him. But he needed to know what else might be going on in the camp. He crept forward, waiting as the woman vanished into the dome. He moved quickly. No signs of dogs, for which he was grateful. A worn track ran between the domes, but frustratingly, he saw no vehicles. No horses, either, but there were enough piles of droppings to show the camp dwellers had a few.

Each shelter he passed was zipped up. Survival pods, he recognized.

Compact, made to be stored and deployed in case of emergencies. During the return, people had used them for years while building what became River City.

He rounded a dome with red patches on top at the end of the lane, searching for a vehicle of any kind. Something large lay covered beneath several camo tarps of digital yellows and browns. A shelter for crops or a workspace, Miles guessed, but pulled over a massive frame. Whatever it was, it was bigger than any of the shelters.

He raised a loose section of tarp. Blinked. It was the last thing he expected to see out in the desert.

A space shuttle.

The craft was a broad-body cigar shape with wings and a split tail fin. It was sunken into the dirt, its landing gear folded or missing. Half of one wing was sheared off, and sections of the fuselage were pockmarked.

Not a Meridian craft, or more exactly, not one the subsidiary corporation Rupert Forge Ltd would manufacture. This was a Caretaker shuttle, Earth or Luna made. Whether the Caretakers were dead or alive, few if any of their shuttles had survived the last confrontation in space, which had shattered the moon bases along with the orbital ring.

Had its final flight been so long ago? Other suspicions crept into his mind. Was this the source of the IFF transponder that had somehow made it to Meridian and then placed on board the Seraph Express, only to be snatched by Dawn Moriti? If so, the device had almost come full circle in its return to the desert.

Mysteries for another time.

Someone ducked out of the nearest dome. Kenji. The gang member was shirtless and wore a bandage across his chest and shoulder. His eyes went wide when he saw Miles. Miles chased him into the dome. Kenji threw a small table at Miles before tripping over a chair.

Miles kicked the chair aside, dropped on top of Kenji, and backhanded him. "How many more of you are here?"

Kenji licked his lips and smiled nervously. "They're coming. They're all coming. He knows where you are."

"Maybe he does. Now I've got a hostage."

Miles used an extension cord to tie Kenji's hands. He sat him at the far wall of the shelter and rummaged for a key to a vehicle or anything useful.

"Your bike or car?"

Kenji stared through his greasy bangs. "He wanted Walker. But now he wants you. He knows. He *knows*, law man. He sees your sins."

"My therapist will be happy. Says I need to open up more."

A quick survey of the dome's interior revealed kitchen supplies, tools, personal effects, and scattered dirty laundry. Five bunks. A com device like the one he had stolen rested on a charger. He set it on the floor and destroyed it.

"That won't make a difference. You're in our world now. Submit and find mercy."

"One more word and I gag you with one of those stinky socks."

He couldn't wait to be found. But taking Kenji with him wasn't a solution. As he glanced out the shelter door, Kenji had gotten to his feet and charged at him, his hands still bound behind his back. They collided and landed on the ground out front. Miles grappled with the man and rolled on top of him.

Kenji was shouting, "Help! He's here!"

The woman who looked like Vaya appeared with a rifle in her hand. She snapped off a shot as Miles scrambled away from Kenji. He almost stumbled as he sprinted towards the cover of the tarps around the shuttle.

Once beneath, he didn't wait to see if anyone was chasing him as he hurried towards the nose of the covered craft. Here were crates with plastic labels and QR codes that Insight wanted to scan. Miles had his weapon out as he emerged from the tarps. Another greenhouse stood next to a second set of moisture collectors. No horses, no vehicles, no flying machines. Getting back to Walker meant going around the camp.

"Marshal Kim," Gabriel said from the radio. "If you're on this channel, please respond. I know you have a radio. We've been tracking you with it. Standing mute will only force me to assume you won't surrender peacefully."

Miles couldn't help himself. "Like you let those militia troopers surrender?"

"You saw that, did you? They were trespassing. I sent a warning."

"You murdered them. There was no trial. It was an execution!"

"They were reminded by radio they were outside of Seraph's jurisdiction. You, too, have enjoyed ample warning. Your prisoner is who I wanted. But now you've assaulted my people. Praise the creator, none died. You're an unwelcome intruder, a soldier of an enemy state."

"You were in Seraph territory when you cut off the fingers of a man who wanted nothing to do with your justice."

"The *camp's* justice. Do you truly not see the difference? I merely uprooted guilt."

"Your people also murdered Ruthie and Dora Alcott and two other people in the desert."

"You'd blame me for any crime under the sun, much like your Meridian progenitors. None of my actions would have been necessary if you inept lawgivers did your job. This isn't a negotiation. Before your flight from Manna, it would have been possible to allow your sins to be pardoned had you cooperated. But aiding the fugitive and the murder of Marshal Jodie? Those crimes are not forgiven. Justice demands a reckoning."

Chapter Twenty-Eight

"Coming for you, law man," Kenji shouted.

His voice might have come from up the hillside or from the rear of the shuttle. The camo tarps around the front formed a spacious work area, where an assortment of old and dismantled machines, vehicles, and appliances lay scattered. A material printer chugged along, emitting a tortured whirr every few moments. Something inside the machine sounded as if it might break at any moment. It was printing what appeared to be a caliper to a wheel brake. The source of the raw materials became apparent as he got a better view of the port side of the shuttle. A section of the fuselage and most of the protective tiles were gone, and the interior was gutted.

A few smaller devices were also making sounds. One was a transformer with power lines running from the shuttle. Was the reactor still functioning? He estimated it would have enough power for a dozen communities like the camp for over a hundred years.

Insight provided a quick review of the shuttle's components and confirmed it held no weapons in a standard loadout. While the spacecraft was the heart of the gang's camp and their survival, it couldn't fly and thus offered Miles little in the way of help with his current situation.

He took cover next to a makeshift workbench where a pharmaceutical printer stood silent.

From here, he had a good vantage point along the sides of the shuttle. He could see through the mesh tarp material well enough for a view of the hill next to him and the desert on the opposite side.

The pharmaceutical printer had its housing removed, and there was no way to know if the device functioned. Again, not useful. The devices were worth their weight in platinum to criminals in River City, and Miles had busted his share of wannabe drug kingpins on the army base who had set up their own narcotic production labs. But an open crate with packets of pills was marked with a Pacific City company's logo.

So Gabriel's gang wasn't in the drug-making business.

A runner raced past across the sand flats. A second vehicle followed. Both vanished around the side of the hill. He checked the radio. Still on, but no one was talking. He cycled through the channels but picked up no chatter. Smart enough to know he was listening.

They came from both sides, moving along the shuttle, heads down and putting to use the ample cover provided by the storage crates. Miles lined up on one of the gang members, Insight drawing a box on them. Once they advanced, he'd have them.

A canister of hissing gas tumbled in from outside the tarp. He dove aside as it spewed forth gray and black smoke. A second and third canister followed. Murky shapes charged at him through the mist. Insight refused to target. Miles fired as a man with a thick neck and tree trunk arms rushed at him. The laser flashed but the man didn't appear to have been struck as he plowed into Miles, taking him to the ground. Miles used the burner as a club, but another gang member appeared through the smoke, smashed something hard against his head, and the world went fuzzy.

The big man twisted Miles' arms back. Someone clamped restraints on his wrists. The smoke grenades continued to spew their contents as two men picked Miles up. They shoved him out from under the tarps, where they were joined by four more. His escorts had their weapons out as they walked him back towards camp.

Kenji was walking bouncily along, a knife in his hands. "Just a piece of him. You know what the law man did to me?"

The big man kept nudging Kenji away. "Touch him before the boss is done with him, you'll regret it."

"You hear that, law man? You'll finally get a taste of it. And then it'll be you and me."

Miles kept quiet, focusing on how many armed men and women

remained around him. The cuffs on his wrists were tight. Step one would be to get them off.

They brought him past the elderly resident in the lounge chairs. He was the center of their attention. An old man clapped and laughed and toasted with his cup. The woman who looked like Jaya had her rifle slung and stared. Miles couldn't tell if he saw anger or loathing.

They passed rows of corn, raised beds of bok choy, squash, and cucumbers, and a small grove of date palms. A group of children sat beneath an open-air tent in a sunken round classroom while a teacher in the center paused mid-lecture as the entourage walked by.

Kenji held the door open, and Miles' guard brought him inside a large storage house stacked high with containers and sacks of goods. The pungent aroma of fermentation caught his nose. To one side of the storage house hung twisted blocks of hanging cheese covered in white mold.

"Strange room for an execution," Miles said.

His muscle-bound guard directed him towards a steel chest freezer long enough to be a coffin. "There's no jail. Sit."

Miles sat. His guard took out a device and started texting. At the door, Kenji was working his knife on a well-worn sharpening stone. When he saw Miles looking, he bared his teeth and mouthed something Miles didn't care to decipher.

The Jaya dead ringer entered, her rifle no longer on her shoulder. "Kenji, go help bring the elders inside. It's getting hot."

"Nah, Lutfi. I'm gonna stay here and make sure he doesn't slip away again."

"Yang's got this. Don't make me ask you a second time."

Kenji made a face, sheathed his blade, and stormed out. She waited for a moment before closing the door and sitting next to Miles. She had a tray with a bowl of water and a folded washcloth. She dipped the cloth in water and dabbed at Miles' face. The towel came away soiled, then she rinsed and continued the process.

The big guard Yang barely registered her presence as a series of replies chimed on his phone.

"Are you injured?" Lutfi asked in a soft voice.

"Bumps and bruises. You tried to shoot me."

"You trespassed into our camp."

"Is this part of Gabriel's ritual? Wash up before an execution?"

"Don't be so dramatic. Nothing's been decided."

"But Gabriel gets to make those decisions, doesn't he? Or will there be a tribunal of your gang to decide my fate?"

"Your fate? I don't know what you've done, marshal. Perhaps it merits punishment. But for now, I intend to care for you. I see no wounds. Water?"

Miles accepted a sip from a cup. The water tasted of cucumber. It barely scratched the lingering acrid flavor of smoke grenade lining his mouth, but it was otherwise delicious.

"You have a sister, don't you?" Miles asked. "The nurse in Manna."

"I have three sisters. Jayakarta's one of them."

"What does she think about what you and your gang do here?"

She shook her head as she put the cup down. "Gang? Is that what you call us? Our *community* has as much right to exist as yours. Seraph, River city—all part of the same hegemony."

"Gabriel has killed Seraph militia."

"Has he? I know nothing about that. If what you say is true, I wonder what circumstances brought that about? Perhaps the same ones that see you intruding in our village. You've come here with your laser weapon and accusations. But I ask you, if I were to appear in Seraph under similar circumstances, what would be my reception?"

"I'm not here to hurt anyone. I have a prisoner. I'm trying to get him back to Seraph. Gabriel and his followers are trying to keep that from happening."

"I've heard about this prisoner. Paxton Walker."

Miles studied her face. "He just escaped from a Seraph jail. How would you have heard?"

"Lutfi," Yang said from the door. "No more talk. He got his water. He's not bleeding. Time for you to go."

She bunched up the towel, placed it on the center of the tray, and rose to leave.

"How did you know about Walker?" Miles pressed.

"Save your strength, marshal. You'll need it. Welcome to Archangel."

Chapter Twenty-Nine

"Where's your prisoner, marshal?"

Gabriel paced before Miles, hat in hand. His thin hair was slicked back and long enough to hang down below his collar. In the light coming through the doorway of the storehouse, he appeared skeletal, the skin around his mouth tight and his cheeks sunken. His left ear was pale white plastic, a cheap prosthetic. Did the gang boss have other augmentations?

"Hiding," Miles said. "Run off by now, I'm sure. They don't pay me enough to be a martyr."

"You speak truthfully. Your voice, your mannerisms. You know it was a mistake to run. Hiding Paxton Walker's location would only condemn you."

He nodded to one of the gang members who had gathered inside. The woman had a slung rifle with a scope, crimson dyed hair, and a green bandana around her head. Was this Carmine? She exited the storehouse and two others fell in behind her.

Miles had been waiting for a little over an hour before the gang appeared in full force. Gabriel had been the first to speak with him. The big guy Yang remained his constant guard, and he hadn't given Miles any opportunity to get free from the cuffs binding his wrists.

"Honesty is an important baseline, wouldn't you agree?" Gabriel asked.

Miles ignored the ache in his back from sitting so awkwardly. "I guess. Neat trick. Rumors the military had empathy modules installed in their interrogators. Makes sense the opposition had them, too. Meridian, for all its countermeasures, could never hold onto secrets."

"People reveal their secrets in many ways, marshal."

"You're a Caretaker, aren't you? Wanted by Meridian even before the war. I may not go back that far, but you do. Looking spry, if I may say so."

"I am old. I was much younger then. You have Meridian military files in that head of yours?"

"Nah. Just an old Insight module in need of an update. Don't even have a current wiki on the state of the world. But I was in the war. And everyone heard the stories when the ring came crashing down."

Gabriel tilted his head to one side and closed his eyes for a moment. "Mankind's greatest achievement. Its greatest vanity. If half the resources for the orbital ring had been spent on restoring Earth, we would live in paradise."

"Bit of a simplification, isn't it?"

"A discussion not worthy of my time."

"Places to be and people to condemn?" Miles asked.

Gabriel's tone grew icy. "I don't rejoice in the correction any more than a father would cherish using the rod. But without it, ruin. I suspect my words are lost here. You murdered a fellow marshal."

"Yeah. And I'll face scrutiny over it if I make it home."

"But the crime was committed outside of Seraph's boundary. Which, like Walker, places you in my authority."

"You didn't have fixed boundaries when you and your Caretakers took control of the ring."

"This again? You claim you have no reference files."

"But everyone returning to Earth heard about what happened. Enough footage got out before the ring's communications got fried. Archangel. The woman who brought me here said that's what you call this place. That was the nickname of the Caretaker regiment who captured the ring. While the rest is sketchy and changes with each telling, the ranking Caretaker officer who survived the takeover spent the next week blowing people out of the airlocks, reading out their sentences across the networks. Even your superior officers were ordering you to stand down, but you didn't listen. Then the reactors got blown and the positioning boosters deactivated. We're reminded of the results when we see the haze of debris in the sky above at night. You want truth? Own what you did."

"That...was a long time ago."

Miles twisted his wrists. If only disconnecting his right arm was easy. "Is there a statute of limitation on mass murder?"

"Those who would steal a world delivered from the brink of ruin and reclaim it only so it might be once again rendered lifeless deserve no mercy."

"Like I thought. You're as big a hypocrite as any exec in Meridian. You at least got your hands dirty."

Kenji came into the storehouse with Walker hobbling ahead of him. "Found him under one of the water tanks."

Walker collapsed on the floor at Gabriel's feet. His nose trickled blood, and one of his eyes was swollen.

"Didn't come quietly," Kenji added.

Gabriel appraised the new prisoner. "Paxton Walker, you stand accused of assisting in the fabrication of counterfeit medical compounds. Prepare to face your victims."

They were brought to the center of camp. Kenji crouched nearby, again playing with his knife. Other gang members were likewise watching as Miles and Walker were forced to their knees. The older residents were arranged nearby on their lounge chairs beneath the palm trees and a canvas for shade.

"I'm not feeling very well," Walker said.

Kenji stepped closer and smacked his head.

Miles glared at him. "Easy, there partner. You've got us. No need for unnecessary roughness."

Kenji belted him, too. Was shaking his hand after the blow, but had caught Miles squarely across his left cheek.

"Enough." Gabriel drank from a bottle of water.

Miles straightened himself, ignoring the ringing in his head from the blow. "Mind telling me what happened to my dog?"

Gabriel appeared not to have heard the question. He leaned to whisper in Yang's ear. The big guy went to one tent and pushed out another resident who was strapped across the chest to a wheelchair. The man's emaciated body didn't appear to have the strength to sit upright. Tremors ran through him, his jaw was twisted, and his head lolled to one side. His thin arms were curled up and pressed against his stomach.

Yang removed a backpack from the rear of the wheelchair and brushed dust from it before handing it to Gabriel.

Gabriel stepped in front of the elderly group and undid the cord tying the pack closed. "Is everyone here?"

"Everyone that's going to make it," Yang said.

Lutfi was helping the older woman who had been tottering around earlier to a chair. Miles' dog appeared next to them. The old woman's eyes lit up and she grabbed him into a hug that the dog endured as it tried to lick her face.

"That answers that question," Miles said. "The little traitor. My knees are starting to hurt. How much longer we going to be?"

Gabriel pulled a box from the backpack. He then crouched to kiss the man with the tremors before holding up the box.

"What you see here is death," Gabriel said. "Death to any who took this poison. A betrayal to those who trusted it would help treat them." He pointed at Walker. "And this is the man who sold it to us."

He dumped the box of wrapped medical ampules. The cartridges landed in a pile in front of Walker.

"I don't understand," Walker said. "It wasn't me."

Gabriel crouched next to him and leaned close. "Only truth here. I smell your lies."

"Foxglove and his partner did it. I just faked credentials so Foxglove could get the ingredients from the supplier."

"Ingredients that, when used in the pharma printer, resulted in antibiotics, radiation treatments, and other life-saving drugs that were useless."

"They...they told me it was all getting sold to Meridian! Meridian machines would detect the faulty compounds. We would have made our money, the hospital insurance would have covered the loss, no one was supposed to get hurt!"

"People *did* get hurt. These are some of the survivors. My son's anti-seizure medications nearly killed him."

"I'm sorry! I was in jail for this. I confessed everything to the prosecutor and pleaded guilty."

"Yet you were coming out to my desert to meet your partners in crime."

"I didn't mean for this to happen. Foxglove promised me no one would die or get sick."

Miles got to his feet. "Gabriel, that's enough of this. He's already serving a sentence. Walker isn't hiding anything, except lying to me about who he was meeting. If there's fresh evidence he did more, he'll pay for it. But executing people with no evidence isn't justice."

"The heart bears witness," Gabriel said with a gleam in his eye.

"You have some kind of empathetic augmentation in your head? You know those things don't work, right? They're as fake as the drugs you got sold. But from what I'm hearing, Walker acted as a forger. Nothing more, nothing less."

Kenji approached and pushed Miles back to his knees.

"Where does it end?" Miles continued. "The idiot who sold the goods to Foxglove without checking what they'd be used for? Every person who failed to do their job in keeping this kind of thing from happening? The software developer for your old machine that couldn't detect counterfeit ingredients? Let's rent a bus, head to Seraph and then River City and round up the suspects."

Gabriel clenched his jaw. "It doesn't end. Everyone receives justice. Some sooner than they'd like."

"You already got two of the criminals who did this. Two dead by your hands."

"You don't know when to shut up," Kenji said.

He was about to strike Miles when Gabriel held up a hand.

"Explain yourself," Gabriel said. "You alluded to them before. Of what dead do you speak?"

"Foxglove. Name might be Eddie. I haven't learned his last name. And Ruthie Alcott's tool pusher Ivan. Both murdered, with guilty signs on them."

Gabriel's expression had become serene, but a storm raged behind his eyes.

"How can you not know?" Miles asked. "What game are you playing?"

"What I know and don't doesn't concern you. Think of your own crimes, marshal. But the time has come for Paxton Walker to face what he has done."

Kenji got Miles into a headlock before he could do anything. Fixed Miles in place.

Gabriel held out his arms towards Walker. "This criminal needs a taste of his bad medicine." He embraced the accused man. "I feel your fear and your guilt. Let it go. Let it drain from you. Your pain will be a poultice. Your grief, a redemption. But look on the faces of those who suffered. And through their eyes, the souls of those in the ground judge you."

Walker was crying. When Gabriel released him, Yang was there to hold onto Walker.

"Lutfi?" Gabriel said. "The injector."

She remained motionless next to the elderly residents. "I'm having no part in this."

"No part? You saw what happened. You cleaned the messes. This satisfies our community's demand for right. For everyone who has lost and felt pain because of his actions."

"This is cruel. It won't bring my mother back."

Gabriel nodded to another guard, who went off and returned a moment later with Lutfi's medical bag. He produced an injector and showed it to Gabriel.

"Ten shots," Gabriel said. "One for each death."

The guard grabbed a handful of the spilled ampules and loaded one into the injector. He walked over to the struggling Walker, pressed the injector to his shoulder, and fired. It hissed, then the spent cartridge popped. Walker's shriek was muffled as another guard forced a rag into his mouth and brought him to the ground. The guard with the injector loaded a new ampule.

Miles tried to wrench away from the hands holding him. "Stop it! You'll kill him!"

The guard delivered the second dose. And the third. It kept going, each hiss of the injector followed by Walker's increasingly weak mewling.

After the tenth injection, they released Walker. He was quivering, face in the dirt. Foam trickled from his mouth, and his eyes rolled up.

"Walker!" Miles called. "Gabriel, what did you give him?"

"The poison he gave those poor souls."

"He's dying. Help him."

"The community has spoken. Justice has been served. Now to your crimes." He came close and took Miles' face into his hands. "Such sights you've seen. So much violence. Your perfect body ruined and grafted with rough steel by masters who would see you give more than what was promised to them."

Gabriel inhaled and held his breath for a moment before letting it out.

"Justice, marshal. Despite your words, you believe. Your murder of Marshal Jodie was in self-defense, even as you doubt yourself and wonder if it could have transpired differently. It couldn't. Let your conscience be at rest. Your sole guilt is standing in my way. You trespass and would disrupt our lives. But for the crimes with which this court has convened, you are innocent. What remains to be discussed is what to do with you. Because you cannot be allowed to ever leave Archangel."

Chapter Thirty

They dragged Miles back to the storehouse. The air conditioning was blowing full force and barely keeping the outside heat at bay.

He was left alone on the floor. Failing to get comfortable with his wrists still cuffed, he leaned against a wall and got to his feet.

A quick tour revealed nothing useful. If he wanted an exit besides the door, the walls were solid. He'd need free hands and a tool to cut through. No weapons to be found unless he intended to swing a block of cheese with his teeth.

Walker was gone. Even if the militia made its way south in force, no one knew where Miles was. How many other camps were there like this one? They'd report him as another officer of the law gone missing. Seraph's patrol limits would be underscored, the dead patrol mourned, and he would be forgotten.

Insight prodded him with a reminder. He had signed a life insurance document back at the office, but the fine print required proof of death. Dillan wouldn't receive a single credit unless Miles' body was found.

Shut up, Insight.

Voices outside.

He walked to the center of the storehouse, abandoning the idea he might play sick. Doubted they'd care.

Lutfi entered with her bag and a basket. Carmine was acting as sentry. The dog slipped in before the guard could close the door. The dog gave Miles a cursory sniff as he headed off to inspect the dry goods. A fresh bandage covered the wound on the animal's side.

When Carmine tried to enter, Lutfi stopped her.

"I'm tending to his wounds," Lutfi said. "I'll require privacy."

"Why bother?" Carmine asked.

"Because it's my job. Out."

Miles allowed himself to be led to the bench. "I'm not injured."

"You're still dehydrated. When's the last time you ate?"

He didn't argue as she unpacked the basket and fed him flatbreads smeared with bean paste that tasted like salty glue. The dried dates were sweet and good, and she gave him water and dabbed his lips.

"They're going to execute you," she said plainly.

"No new trial? Gabriel run out of ideas for his show, or is everyone sick of it?"

"He differentiates between war and justice. Your incursion, the militia patrol, you shooting his disciples at Manna—acts of an enemy combatant. Don't mock him. He's sincere in his beliefs."

"Which you don't share," Miles said. "You mentioned your mother. She died?"

Lutfi nodded. "There's more cancer down here than anyplace else. High radiation. Both the ground and the air are sick. The drugs my mother took wouldn't have cured her, but they would at least have eased her pain. When they failed and we discovered the ingredients had been tampered with..."

"I'm sorry."

"Tormenting Walker or anyone else responsible won't bring her or any of the others back."

Miles shook his head. "Then why go along with it?"

"Don't be stupid. You think things are any different in Seraph or River City? Do you get to decide what laws you will and won't abide by?"

"Of course not. This is different. Gabriel is one man deciding what crimes are punishable and how. And like you said: what he does is cruel."

She packed the food away. "Not everyone sees it as you do."

"A last meal for the condemned and your conscience is clean. That's what's important to you."

"Don't make me regret my decision to see you. You're uninvited here.

Your presence promises to disrupt our lives, and we have as much right to exist as you. But I didn't come here to argue. You said something about Foxglove and his associate."

Miles brushed crumbs from his hands. "Gabriel didn't know what I was talking about when I mentioned they had been murdered."

"He must have assumed you were lying, marshal. What do you know about them?"

"His empathy skills must be slipping. It's the truth. I know Walker escaped lockup to go meet Foxglove. He was supposed to get Walker out of the territory and over to New Pacific. But we found Foxglove dead up at a place called High Spring with a guilty sign on him. Same thing with his alleged partner, Ivan. When Gabriel set up court in Manna, I thought he was continuing what he started."

The basket packed, she checked her device. "Gabriel has half his men still looking for them."

"You trying to tell me he didn't kill them?"

"I don't know. But he would have put them on trial first. He believes the accused should face their victims."

"Look, I know you don't owe me anything." Miles thought for a bit, then added, "Tell me about your sister Jaya."

Lutfi sighed. "Younger by three years. Jayakarta was never content to stay in one place. I was surprised to learn she had made a home in one of the camps rather than going back to Seraph. I heard she got into trouble there."

"You're not close with one another," Miles pressed.

"I was upset with her for leaving. When I reached out to her to tell her about our mother, she wouldn't come home to help deal with the others who had fallen sick. We haven't spoken since. She was angry—with me, with Gabriel, with everyone."

"Angry enough to go after the people who poisoned your mother?"

Her face hardened. "I would never believe this."

"She had some drugs in her bag that might have been from your old drug printer. Foxglove—Eddie—had some in his pocket. Is this a coincidence?"

"Our pharma printer works, but good ingredients are scarce. Others in the gang trade with her despite Gabriel forbidding it. My two older sisters and some others are close with her and tell me when I ask about her."

"What's Jaya's take on Gabriel's approach to justice?"

"She's a believer. But she has said it herself that Gabriel doesn't take things far enough. She was always his favorite granddaughter. That doesn't mean she's capable of killing those men."

Miles let the information sink in. Jaya and Lutfi were related to Gabriel. So much of what Jaya had said and done, the attack by Kenji and Rocko. Was it all a ruse? Jaya was part of Gabriel's private campaign for justice in the wastes and had played Miles perfectly.

Lutfi was watching him. "You are perhaps a decent man, marshal."

"I don't have an answer for that. Want me to say that I am?"

"Of course not. It's our actions that prove our worth. As much as it saddens me, if my sister is involved with murders in the name of Gabriel's justice, if you have proof, I'd see her stopped."

She unlocked his cuffs and removed them.

He rubbed life back into his tingling hands. "Help me understand. You don't believe in Seraph law."

"You don't know what I believe. I know that my grandfather's response could prove disruptive, now that Jayakarta has been accused of acting behind his back."

"What will your grandfather do?"

"I don't know how he'll respond. He won't remain idle. He knows his disciples are fond of her, some perhaps viewing her as the future after his passing. His principles will dictate an action. But no one would dare lay a finger on her when it comes to punishment."

"You tell me they're going to kill me, and now you're letting me go. How do you know I'm going to do what you're hoping for?"

She took a knee next to the dog and began examining him. "I don't know. But I don't want to see Jaya hurt."

"Even if it means I might have to kill your grandfather to stop him?"

"Yes."

He approached her to see what she was doing. "I came here to bring a fugitive back," he said. "He's gone. Maybe I take this opportunity to use you as a hostage and get myself out of here alive."

She unlatched the dog's stomach compartment. "You will do what you believe is right. But your prisoner, Paxton Walker, isn't dead. He was breathing when I last checked."

The dog just stared off as if Lutfi were doing something as mundane as brushing down his coat. She pulled a pistol from the dog's insides, considered it for a moment, and handed the weapon to Miles.

Full magazine, clean, safety off, and a round already chambered.

She snapped the stomach compartment closed. "You shouldn't actually feed these robots, even though the makers say it's okay."

"I'll keep that in mind. Where's Walker?"

"My grandfather will leave to go find Jaya after he finishes what he started today. He would never have left those men exposed to the air like you said. The last part of justice is caring for the dead. He took Walker to the cemetery."

Chapter Thirty-One

Too Easy.

Carmine, the sentry, wasn't expecting Miles and didn't call out for help. Miles got her inside the storehouse and, with Lutfi's help, cuffed to the bench and gagged.

A survey of the camp found the horses and vehicles gone, along with the gang. The camp's other residents were out of sight, likely inside their domes.

A compressor or motor rumbled from somewhere nearby.

"The cemetery is to the south," Lutfi said. "I won't go with you unless you force me to."

"I'm not going to do that. You know if I run or if Gabriel kills me, he'll know you helped."

"We stand for our principles. It's all we have out here."

Running would be the smart thing. He wouldn't have Walker slowing him down. No one in Seraph cared about what happened outside their territory. Walker could be written off as escaped or killed during his flight as a fugitive. Miles could construct any narrative. Marshal Barma would take him at his word, and he wouldn't face any repercussions about any of it, including Marshal Jodie's death.

Lutfi gave him a final nod before taking her bag and basket and hurrying off.

With the dog at his side, Miles walked south.

The compressor sounds grew louder as Miles approached the cemetery. Kenji operated a backhoe and was digging out a trench in the middle of a stony yard hedged off by a wall of stacked rocks. Grave markers stood in untidy rows, the wood slats sun bleached, the epitaphs and names faded.

Gabriel stood at the head of the hole, a bundled body at his feet. Rocko was next to him, her rifle slung on a shoulder. She spotted Miles and went for her weapon.

Miles shot her.

She collapsed with the rifle under her.

Gabriel flinched. The dog skittered back from Miles, surprised by the loud report. Kenji didn't appear to notice. He wore protective earmuffs and was having trouble with the control levers as the backhoe trembled and the attached compressor redoubled its thrumming.

Eyes fixed on Miles, Gabriel had his hands half raised at his waist. He wore two pistols on his hips.

"Don't," Miles shouted. "Tell Kenji to shut that machine down."

Kenji finally realized what was happening and almost tumbled out of the seat. The compressor motor softened as it idled. Miles motioned for Kenji to join Gabriel. Kenji climbed down and stepped past Rocko, who was clutching a blossoming wound on her side.

Arms out, Gabriel licked his teeth. "It appears *two* of my granddaughters have chosen a disappointing path."

"You made it easy when you've got everyone guessing what they need to do to toe the law in your kingdom."

"We serve the same master whether or not you know it, marshal. We push against chaos with all our might, knowing that one slip and we are lost."

"I have no idea what you're talking about. Kenji, unwrap Walker."

Kenji crouched and tugged away the shroud. Walker was visibly breathing but appeared comatose.

Miles kept the pistol leveled. "It wasn't enough to shoot him full of bad drugs? But burying him alive?"

"He was never going to wake up," Gabriel said.

"So you bury him and execute me. Then what was the plan after?"

"Find my wayward granddaughter."

"And put her in a hole too?"

"Of course not. Her desire for justice is as strong as mine. She only needs to be reined in. Guided. Trained in the way of things, like you were by Marshal Jodie."

"What happens if she refuses?" Miles asked.

"You need to think of your own fate. Walker's has been decided. Your actions and presence here are unwelcome. Your death would serve as a continuing warning against a state we don't recognize. Another marshal gone missing, and the status quo is maintained. If you leave now, I give you my word you will be allowed to make it back to Seraph's arbitrary boundary without harm. Return to your masters. Let them know the fate waiting future incursions. That serves both of us."

"Walker's coming with me."

Gabriel chuckled. "How far will you make it? If we don't catch you again, the desert will. Earth demands its price. The growing communities of man spreading like tumors will again lose while we faithfully trim our wicks and wait and serve. Leave Walker to me. Your heart demands it. You saw what evils his actions caused. Every transgressor who walks free under the guise of due process is a stone in your gut and rising bile in your throat."

"I take a pill for that."

"You mock me, but my words resonate. As the cursed earth delivers her crop of thorns, even the most assured of the returnees will see a new way must be taken lest a second fall occurs."

"Maybe you're right. Rebuilding means suffering through wrong choices and sorting out bad actors. What happens when your camp isn't just a hundred people but a thousand? Ten thousand? You going to officiate over every grievance, cutting off fingers and burying people alive for whatever pricks your brain as offensive? Hard pass. Both of you back up."

They edged away from Walker. Miles moved around the lip of the grave and crouched next to his fugitive. He patted his cheek and was rewarded by Walker looking up at him with bleary eyes.

"Stop...hitting me."

"Come on. You've got to get up."

He eased Walker to a sitting position, but the man was deadweight. When Walker sagged back, Miles' weapon hand drooped. Kenji went for it, ducking behind the nearest grave marker while pulling a needle gun from the back of his belt. Miles hit the dirt as a spray of flechettes ripped through the air. Miles squeezed off several shots. The grave marker splintered. Kenji groaned. The high whine of the needle gun cut out as the man toppled.

Gabriel was on the move as well, taking cover behind the pile of newly dug dirt. He had both his pistols drawn.

Miles pivoted and snapped off a shot before rolling for cover behind the backhoe. Insight kept trying to provide a target. Miles dismissed the interface. With the unfamiliar pistol, it was useless. A bullet pinged off the steel, forcing him to pull his legs in.

How many times had he fired? Hadn't been paying attention. Didn't want to waste the precious second to reopen Insight. Gabriel had two weapons and only needed to wait Miles out for the few minutes it would take until whatever other gang members were near to come running.

The backhoe stood on three legs. The rear compartment contained the engine. A housing in front of the seat held the controls. Miles held his weapon high and popped off three more rounds before the pistol clicked empty. He rose as he fired, reaching for the controls.

It had been decades since he had last operated anything like the machine, but he took a chance with a lever and threw it to the right. The raised bucket swung towards Gabriel, forcing him away from the cover of the dirt pile.

Rocko lay a couple of arm's lengths away.

Miles went for her rifle, yanking it from her and pointing it. Gabriel was coming around the backhoe when Miles and Gabriel fired simultaneously. Miles winced as something struck him, a crisp slap to his shoulder. Gabriel fell to a knee. Miles pulled the trigger again but the rifle only clicked. It had a bolt action that took a precious moment to work so the weapon could shoot again.

Gabriel still had his guns but both hands had drooped to his side. His lips quivered. A dark stain grew on his shirt. No words came as he keeled forward.

Miles rose on shaking legs, keeping the weapon trained on the three fallen gang members. No one was moving. He went to the compressor and turned the key, shutting it down.

As the rumble and the last echoes of the rifle died away, Miles' ears continued to ring. Breathing too fast. He fought back a wave of nausea. Rocko was watching him but appeared to do little else but keep her hand on her wound. Kenji lay still. No one else was coming, at least for the moment.

He pulled off his shirt and confirmed he had been hit. Two lacerations bled, one on his shoulder near the metal joint of his right arm, the other on his neck. The latter, if a centimeter or two in, would have finished him.

He brought Insight back online. It knew the rifle. His new weapon held ten shots. No way of knowing if Rocko had started with a full ten without checking. He made a quick search of Rocko, then Kenji, and finally Gabriel. Coins, ammo, radios and mobile devices, binoculars, a water bottle. He took a keyring off Kenji.

At the far side of the cemetery, past a stand of shrubs, waited a horse and a desert runner.

Miles wasn't sure if he had the strength to pick Walker up. "You can walk."

"I think so."

"It wasn't a question. I can't carry you. There's our ride. Get up or get left behind."

Chapter Thirty-Two

Miles was fading. He kept blinking himself awake, wishing the pain in his shoulder would either go away or hurt more so he wouldn't fall asleep behind the wheel. But a few hard blinks and Walker shouting at him did little to stave off slumber.

"Anything in the glove box?" Miles asked. "Stim? Water?"

Walker checked. "Chewing gum."

The gum tasted like sweetened wax and felt like it was going to pull his teeth out, but Miles worked the wad of old candy and kept his eyes fixed on the track of desert ahead of them. The headlights felt small and dim and the night an opaque wave set to crash on top of them and sweep them into an abyss.

Gabriel's camp lay hours behind them. They had avoided the road and anything that looked like it served as a trail. Deep ruts in the landscape had them continually turning north. The gang couldn't be everywhere, but there might only be so many passages through the canyons.

Walker had done a serviceable job of bandaging Miles' wounds. The cut in his neck was merely a scrape, but a flechette remained lodged in his shoulder and continued to ache. Time for surgery later.

With both hands on the dashboard, Walker stared through the windshield at the dark desert before them. He kept gasping and continued to reach for the steering wheel every time Miles drifted. At one precipitous drop-off, Walker grabbed it and turned hard as the runner tilted and slid sideways before Miles got them back on flat ground.

"We can't keep driving in the dark like this," Walker said.

Miles ignored him.

The radio on the dash provided little but static. On one channel, they heard a snippet of chatter that lasted only seconds before yielding to dead air.

When they drove into what turned out to be a box canyon with no outlet, Miles turned around and began driving the opposite direction. But then he stopped the runner abruptly and backed the vehicle up.

"What are you doing?" Walker asked.

"You're right."

"I am?"

"We're going to wait for the morning. Then we continue when we can see where we're going. Stay in the car. Watch the dog."

"Where will you be?"

Miles took the rifle and climbed out. "Around."

Insight volunteered more information than needed about the Meridian military surplus runner they had taken. Miles was used to ignoring the infodumps, but still found himself muttering.

"Just shut up, Insight."

His sleepy brain kept thinking about the radio in the vehicle. It held a distress beacon along with a transponder. Had they been tracked since leaving Archangel? At first glance, the gang appeared to be throwbacks of a bygone era, but now he knew they weren't Luddites. They had enough firepower to take out an armored vehicle, owned a medical printer, and used a Caretaker shuttle reactor as a power supply. The shuttle would have a communications suite to monitor a vehicle's radio beacon.

Miles was about to pop the hood and disconnect the radio from the power supply, but paused.

"Insight? Spot anything that moves. And keep me from falling asleep."

With that, he climbed to a perch with a good view of the moon, the runner, and the mouth of the canyon.

With each passing hour, he second guessed the wisdom of his decision. The gang's leader was dead. He needed sleep if they had any hope of driving out of the desert alive. And for one heart-squeezing moment, he had forgotten whether he had left the keys in the runner.

What would stop Walker from slipping behind the wheel and abandoning him?

A quick pat of a pocket confirmed he still held the keys and wasn't losing his mind.

He allowed himself to lean back and get comfortable, ignoring the gnawing chill and falling into the routine of watching the night, nearly nodding off, and being prodded awake by the computer inside his brain.

They appeared at dawn.

One buggy, one motorcycle. The buggy first, which stopped at the mouth of the box canyon as the motorcycle raced forward. It sped towards their stolen runner and pulled up in front of it, sending up a cloud of dust. The rider was off his bike and pulled a shotgun from a saddlebag.

The sun was rising behind Miles. The biker would be blind if he tried to look up at his position. Miles leaned across a rock and planted the butt of the rifle against his shoulder close enough to his wound to cause it to throb. Too much dust. He kept both eyes open. The buggy remained idling a hundred meters off.

"Come on, buddy," he murmured.

He needed both vehicles out of commission if they were going to make a getaway.

"Out of the car!" the biker shouted.

He walked around the front of the runner, shotgun aiming. Walker wasn't getting out. If he did, Miles would have no choice but to either shoot or let the gang take him. He sighted on the biker. Still too much dust, but thanks to Insight, he had a target. It would be sloppier than if he had his burner.

The buggy engine revved. Miles didn't lose focus on the biker. The buggy rolled to a stop behind the bike. Two men got out, both with sidearms. Insight obliged and provided each a red square.

Miles wanted to know if there was a driver still in the buggy. Pushed the thought aside as the biker tried the door and then smashed at the window. Walker was inside the runner and screaming.

The window popped into a glaze of spiderweb.

Another pushed the biker aside and raised his pistol. The dust cloud had shifted. Miles switched targets and squeezed the trigger. The rifle bucked, slamming his shoulder as thunder exploded from the barrel.

Insight deselected his target, leaving him two squares. He worked the bolt, shifted aim to the second gang member out of the buggy, fired, slid another cartridge into the breech.

Two down.

His last target was moving. The biker hid behind his motorcycle. Miles got him in his sights, but the man was on the move, rolling the bike along while keeping low. Miles put a round into the engine. The biker threw the vehicle down and scrambled into a ditch.

A quick survey of the ground around the desert runner confirmed two down, and the biker had dropped his shotgun. Still might have a sidearm. But no one else appeared to be inside the buggy.

Miles descended from his boulder. He kept the rifle ready to shoot as he made it to the runner.

"Walker, you alive?"

"Marshal Kim?"

"Who else were you expecting? Were you hit?"

"I'm okay."

Miles shouted at the ditch. "Hey, you. You've got sixty seconds to start running. After that, I come for you. If I see a weapon, you're dead."

A five-count elapsed before the biker was up and tripping over himself as he sprinted off past the buggy. Miles watched him leave before patting down the other two gang members. He unloaded their sidearms before tossing them away.

Walker emerged from the runner. "Y-you used me as bait."

"I didn't know they'd come. Get back in the car."

"I have to pee."

Miles waited for Walker to finish his business. Once Walker was back in the vehicle, Miles inspected the bike. With a bullet hole in the engine, it wasn't going anywhere. A search of the buggy revealed a large radio and a trio of long whip antennae strapped to the dome of the roof. It had a transmitter and repeater.

With it, the gang had a mobile communication hub. Without it, the gang still in the field would be isolated like him.

If they had more than one car like this one, he had no way to know. No doubt they would have good communications this far south with their home base and shuttle, but they'd face problems with their radios in the canyons to the north.

He needed to go. Instead, he climbed into the buggy and turned the radio on. Once finished, he took the keys from the ignition and considered which cables to undo to disable the transmitter. He settled on putting a couple of bullets into it.

"What were you shooting at?" Walker asked when Miles returned to the desert runner.

"Leveling the playing field." He handed Walker a baggy with what looked like homemade granola bars he had found in the buggy. "Here's breakfast. Now strap in. It's going to be a long drive to get you home to Seraph."

Chapter Thirty-Three

The front door to Ruthie's house stood ajar. Miles pushed it open without a sound and walked inside. Jaya sat in the atrium with one of Ruthie's ledgers on her lap and a cup of steaming tea in hand. When she spotted him, she almost spilled.

"Marshal Kim?"

Miles carried the rifle in one hand. "Are you armed?"

"Do I need to be? I'm surprised to see you."

"I'm sure you are. It was a near thing. You may have heard: your grandfather is dead."

Her mouth was tight as she nodded.

"You probably also heard I met your sister Lutfi and visited your old camp to the south. I'm sorry about what happened to your mother."

"It was a tragedy. But you're safe."

"Yeah. So is Paxton Walker. He'll be back in a Seraph jail. Thought you should know. Figured you'd be pleased to hear."

She almost choked on her words. "I thought he had been killed."

"Not for you or the gang's lack of trying. Your grandfather administered his version of justice and shot him full of old drugs. Your sister saved him. That should make you happy, right?"

"He's a criminal."

"Who's already serving a sentence and will serve some more after his escape. But if you have firsthand knowledge about his crimes involving the counterfeit drugs Foxglove's ring sold, you could be a witness to additional charges and testify against him."

She was breathing hard, as if hyperventilating. Whispered, "Only to see him walk free in a few months."

"It'll be longer than that. But you're not going to do it. You wanted him for yourself, didn't you? Like Foxglove? Like Ivan? Were Ruthie and Dora involved? At least your grandfather had his trial. You became judge and jury and executioner. How much of his gang are really yours?"

She snapped the ledger closed. "Are you here to arrest me?"

"It's what happens to murderers."

"How many men and women did you kill in the past two days, including one of your own?"

Miles didn't want to think about Marshal Jodie. He scanned the room and confirmed she had no weapon in sight.

"If you're going to arrest me, then do it," she said. "But you wouldn't be wasting time talking if that was your intention. You have no proof."

"I'm sure once we look, we'll find something."

"Bring your forensic team, then," she said. "The law is suddenly interested when it has a criminal to protect. How much did Walker pay you?"

"Nothing. Manna is in Seraph territory. There's a lot to unravel here. You're where the investigation starts. I'm guessing if I search your home in camp, I'll find a radio. It might still be tuned to one of the frequencies used by your grandfather's gang."

She scoffed. "Coincidence, if such a radio could be found. You'll find no witnesses in Manna to back up any of your claims. Every resident is obeying the law."

"Bold claim. You're the one sifting through a dead woman's belongings."

"Ruthie Alcott's tragic death while defending Manna has left me in the position to care for her effects, along with what details she had on managing the camp. The people who live here want to live here. Those that are unhappy can find another camp. Manna needs someone who will lead it, not just be content to let criminals run things."

The transformation on her face was complete. The kind eyes and softness of the woman he had first encountered were gone, replaced with a granite-like expression and a cold-blooded gaze.

"Where are Ruthie and Dora Alcott's bodies?" he asked.

"Another accusation? I'm certain I don't know."

"You believe you can hold your grandfather's gang together while satisfying their lust for extreme justice. I saw scared people at the trial here despite their masks. Most won't move on like you say. They'll do what they have to so they can avoid losing a finger or getting beaten down by their neighbor."

"Manna lies in Seraph territory. It will be a peaceful camp. I intend to make sure of it."

He could tell by her tone he wouldn't get more out of her, and certainly not a confession. He had no leverage.

"Plan on running the gang from here?" he asked.

"I don't lie. Manna will not be a problem. I sense you remain ill at ease. My grandfather told us a story once. He liked stories. This parable he never told a second time, but it was memorable, because when he related it, my mother left the house until it was finished.

"A king in feudal China waged war against a barbarian warlord. The barbarian had the steppes and mountains and was the master of horse and mobility. But the king lived safely behind the walls of a mighty fortress with his army. They fought for ten years, the king secure and able to retreat and rest. It was a standstill. One day, the king listens to his advisors on how to gain a victory. His advisors tell the king to stop chasing the barbarian army and instead go after his villages, and not just his, but even the places loyal to the king who were the victims of the barbarians. So the king did just so. He burned everything in the surrounding land. That winter, the barbarians starved. By spring, the barbarian warlord sued for peace.

"The king won. The warlord was humbled and captured and placed in chains inside the castle dungeon, his men executed, his people subjugated. Over the next decade, the barbarian tribes slowly recovered, traded under unfair conditions, and paid every tribute and tax. After the ten years of peace, they could even come in person to the markets at the fortress. The captured warlord was dying and was granted a visitor. His son came, disguised as a monk who would transcribe his last words. By then, the king too was old and careless and missed the fact the son pretending to be a monk had a forged copy ready of the barbarian warlord's last words. Harmless meanderings, a death poem, nothing of interest.

"The warlord died. But then the son carries the barbarian warlord's actual message out beneath his robes and shares them with his people. Each week when they come to market, every man, woman, and child removes one stone from the fortress. From the roadbed, the causeway, a wall, a tower. One stone taken by every visitor. After another ten years, the king is now on his deathbed when a surprise attack from a horde of barbarians sends his army reeling. Like in the previous war, they hide behind the walls. The last thing the king sees is his weakened fortress crashing around him by a gust of wind."

Miles had been listening patiently. "You want me to take something from this story?"

Her old smile was back, its warmth returned. "Manna will pose no problems. Now, unless you're arresting me, I have a lot of work to do. Is there anything else?"

Chapter Thirty-Four

Marshal Barma waited outside. He sat on the side runner of a Red Banner militia buggy, his jacket off and his hand cannon dangling from the shoulder holster.

The driver and another guard were head-to-toe in tactical armor. They carried carbines and were scanning the camp and the surrounding rocks. They also kept giving Miles sidelong glances.

Barma was chewing on one of Glenda's foil-wrapped sandwiches and feeding Miles' dog scraps.

"I told you he doesn't need to eat," Miles said.

"That's just negative thinking, Kim. Imagine if everyone treated robots like that. You'd be hungry. So let me give this good boy his treats."

"I'll have to scrape him out later."

Barma flipped a piece of synthetic meat into the air. The dog caught it.

"I see you don't have your suspect," Barma said.

"We have little in the way of evidence. And she didn't confess."

"They're going through her home right now. They might come up with something. By the way, you carrying that rifle has the boys nervous."

Both the militia troopers glanced away when Miles turned their direction. He kicked a small rock and did his own scan of the camp. More than a few of the residents lingered outside their homes or were watching through windows. He couldn't believe many of them were eager to have them there. But then he couldn't believe many truly wanted to make Gabriel's exercise in jurisprudence a regular thing. Would that take a more extreme form if Jaya was taking the lead?

Eddie "Foxglove" Proctor and Ivan Volodin hadn't been given a trial.

Miles slid the rifle into the back of the buggy and joined Barma. "So the marshal service provides sidearms like yours?"

"Bought this one myself. But yes, we have a modest budget and a small armory to draw from. It was all in the employment package."

"Didn't read it."

"Make sure you mention you lost your burner in your report. Best if you carry nothing for now until I can digest what happened."

"You want me to go over it again? Ask Walker."

"You're going to go over it as many times as I tell you to. And I will ask Walker once we get back. They just received him at the lockup, and he's getting a nice, cool, isolated cell where no one will mess with him. You getting to talk to Jaya is a courtesy."

"I'm not hiding anything. You'll get to review our conversation once we get back and I upload it for you. She's probably the one who summoned Gabriel and his followers here. She had two people murdered, even if she didn't touch either of the victims. Walker would have been the third. Even if you can't get anything to stick to her, you round up enough of the gang, someone will flip."

Barma considered the remaining bite of sandwich before handing it over to the dog. "Yeah, well, that's a problem. No one can seem to find any of the gang."

"How far south are the Red Banner patrols going?"

"Seraph limit. No further."

Not even getting out of the canyons.

Miles tried to keep his rising frustration out of his voice. "Of course you're not going to find them if that's as far as you go. Their base is the camp they call Archangel. I showed you the map."

"You did. And it's out of bounds. Orders from Sheriff Vaca after word got to her about the lost Red Banner patrol and Marshal Jodie."

"You can't just let them go to ground and regroup."

"That's what's happening. Look, Kim, I'm going to push for a response, but it won't be today. It's how I got Red Banner to be our ride for this in the first place. They're champing for payback, and I need to keep that in check so it doesn't turn into a bloodbath before they roll into every scrapper and sand grubber camp within two hundred clicks and start knocking heads."

"You have the plot graph from my Insight module. Locations of not only Archangel, but where the bodies were found. It also shows the watering hole where I left Marshal Jodie."

"Got word just before we made it here. Jodie wasn't there."

Had the gang taken the body? "How'd you get a patrol unit there so fast?" Miles asked. "I thought you said we were staying in Seraph limits."

"We are. I contacted a source in a mining camp not far from there. Connection was bad, but they got a text out. Marshal Jodie's body was gone."

"You trust this source?"

Barma chuckled as he crumpled the foil wrapper. "'Course not. But that's the world down here. It's the job, Kim. And you got one hell of a baptism."

"You believe my report."

"It's all I got. Things'll be dicey for a bit while we poke around. Sheriff Vaca and the mayor will weigh in once we get back. Community will cry and whine for us to get tough on the settlements to the south. We'll hear from some camps wanting extra patrols. Our office gets to do the Wally-Wally-Three-Step to keep things from boiling over and blowing up. The question for you is where do you want to land?"

"You're still offering me a job."

The big marshal shrugged. "You screwed up big time. Shooting Jodie? It's hard to know what to believe." He stared off for a moment. "You know we're shorthanded. I'll go over your reports. If I can get anything to stick to Jaya, she'll be brought in. You're a smart man, Kim. If you did Marshal Jodie dirty, you know you'll have to deal with me. But there's no upside to you even confessing if it didn't go down like you said. So this Gabriel. He'd have to be pretty old to be the Caretaker officer who brought down the ring."

"Insight has his picture. Without DNA or prints, I can't say for certain."

"Even the picture in the report will make its rounds. You'll have to decide how much detail to put about this Gabriel. It would be something the newsfeeds will eat up if word gets out. Which it will."

"You're saying don't put it in the report."

Barma stood and brushed crumbs from his shirt. "Like your application forms, you have the leeway to provide speculation once you put down all the pertinent facts. By the way, I filled in your name in all the places you left it blank. Lee Chul-Moo, at least in the documentation. File that away in your tickle box."

They rode in the back with the dog between them. The driver took them to the top of Manna's main drag, where they waited for the other two patrol units to join them before heading north.

Miles had time to think since meeting up with Barma and handing off his prisoner. Did Barma need him out of desperation? It explained Marshal Jodie. A lawman past his prime who had been shaken by their ordeal enough to threaten a fellow marshal and be willing to surrender their prisoner to a gang of criminals.

Miles wondered about his own actions. Shooting down the gang members who had been trying to kill them didn't bother him, or at least wouldn't until he was back in his hotel room and trying to sleep. Then the ghosts could come. But his acts of violence had taken place in a stretch of desert where there was no law. Did Gabriel, Jaya, and the gang at Archangel have as much right to declare law as he did?

Barma stared out the window at the passing scenery. "Hell of a first week, Kim. As far as your missing gun, I'm pretty sure there are a couple of decent burners in the locker back at the office. They might even have a battery that keeps its charge."

"Was thinking about a standard slug thrower," Miles said.

"Old school? I like it."

"Sometimes older is better."

Chapter Thirty-Five

The walk to the crest of the plateau was easier than the first time, but not by much. At least Santabutra Sin wasn't running. Miles had the dog on a leash, and it tugged every so often, but otherwise remained content to lead by the length of the nylon cord.

It was late afternoon. The sun had already vanished behind an overcast, gray front rolling in from the west. They passed a couple of groups of hikers on their way down, Santabutra waving to each. Up at the top, Miles took the dog off the leash. They watched as the animal made its rounds, inspecting every inch of soil.

He had left little out of the story. Santabutra had listened without comment and only a few questions for clarification.

"It's amazing people live like that in the desert camps," she said. "And not just live, but thrive."

"From the residents I've seen in the Bright Blocks neighborhood, it might be easier in the desert."

"Except for the pack of religious zealots looking to root out moral turpitude."

Miles looped the leash in his hand. "Seraph has its own gangs who take their toll. But religion plays a role. Jaya leads a Purity group in the Manna bar. I didn't have time to see much in the other camps to the south, but it could be how she's swayed at least part of Gabriel's gang to follow her."

"Purity is an old faith. Spacers, returnees, Caretakers follow it. I pray Purity on Sundays with one of my girlfriends."

"I didn't know that."

"Why should you? I don't talk about it. It brings me peace and comfort. I'm not running around inflicting judgments on my neighbors. Was Gabriel really the Butcher of the Ring?"

"Barma wants to know that, too. If it makes you sleep better, yes. And now he's gone."

"I sleep pretty well as it stands. But word will get out if it was. People talk, including those in the camps down south. It might get you some attention you don't want."

They took in the scenery of the city below before strolling across the plateau for the view of the hills. The main road out of town was visible. A handful of trucks and cars sped along, heading towards or away from Seraph. From the distance, they looked like toys moving in slow motion.

"You keeping the job?" she asked.

"Gotta eat and support my lavish lifestyle."

"Easier ways to make credits. You said yourself you can make ends meet as a security guard. That doesn't require you to face down bandits willing to go toe-to-toe with a marshal. I'm guessing most were younger than you. You got lucky none of them had implants."

"True. Maybe I believe in trying to keep the peace. I'm just hitting a wall on knowing if what we're doing counts towards building Seraph into more than just a big version of Manna. The camp functions with no help from us."

"It's not peace if it's based on fear of when the next sham trial fires up."

"Seraph isn't as overtly brutal. But most of the people down there go about their day keeping their head down so they don't get hassled."

"The Yellow Tigers aren't taking people's fingers for jaywalking."

Miles let a silence settle over them. Breathed it in. The dog had something cornered in a bush but was making no headway in flushing it.

"Who says our justice is right?" Miles asked.

"I'm not that philosophical. It gets in the way of accomplishing anything. My militia does what we have to so things run. We don't blindly follow orders. There's oversight, even if it's frustrating, corrupt, and sometimes grinds things to a halt. But we stop people from hurting others more often than not. If I do my job, I keep the crooks and politicians from tearing the whole thing down. In a perfect world, the law, as written, would apply to the lowliest grunt and the highest executive. But it wasn't that way with Meridian and it's not like that in Seraph. Our law is better than no law. So my Yellow Tigers enforce it here. The marshals do their part in the camps at the fringes."

"You always this certain?"

"Tomorrow's Monday," she said. "Ask me tomorrow evening and I'll tell you a few new lies. But it's the good cops who never stop questioning. That's who I want protecting me when I'm sitting on my porch in my rocking chair."

"That's it, isn't it? It's the home we want. I want that for Dillan and Zoe. I want it for you. I'll work towards that. Maybe I'll decide it's what I want, too."

"That's sweet. I know you're not asking me permission or need my blessings to stay on as a marshal. It's your choice. After this week, you know the risks. You had us worried, though. What did Dillan say?"

"I didn't share specifics of what happened. He hates me coming on board with the marshals, but he won't tell me that. After what happened with the Meridian agents, he'd prefer I take a service job that won't get me shot. But Seraph's my home. This is what I'm good at."

"It's a hard balance when we have loved ones to think about. But Miles? I'm glad you shared what you did with me."

She wrapped his arm with her own, and they watched the sun peer through a window in the clouds.

He looked at her. The almost invisible freckles on her cheeks. Her black eyes.

She smiled and met his gaze. "What?"

He leaned close. "I'd like to kiss you."

"Is that where we are in our relationship? Do I need to worry about getting a shock?"

"Why Captain Sin, I believe you stole my line."

I hope you enjoyed The Gallows of Heaven. Your review and a rating mean a lot to me and will help readers find my books.

The Perdition Run continues Miles Kims' adventure.

A simple escort job becomes a deadly hunt.
When an outspoken New Pacific judge is marked for assassination, only Miles Kim stands in the way of a family of high-tech killers-for-hire.

Miles will have to use all his wits and survival skills to protect the judge, a man who has threatened to reveal Miles' identity to the corporation searching for their missing cyborg.

If the assassins win, they're both dead. If the judge lives, Miles' fragile new life in Seraph will be shattered.

Grab your copy of Perdition Run, Book five of the cyberpunk crime and mystery series Old Chrome!

You may also enjoy these science fiction and fantasy novels published by Lucas Ross Publishing

The Minders' War series by Gerhard Gehrke
For Deanne and her correctional facility work crew, the night the stars fell ended everything.
Refuge
The Glass Heretic
The Children of Magus

The Goblin Reign series by Gerhard Gehrke
They razed Spicy's village, kidnapped his sister, and never imagined what one lone goblin would do to get her back!
Goblin
Goblin Apprentice
Goblin Rogue
Goblin War Chief
Goblin Outcast

The Old Chrome series by I.O. Adler
The Seraph Engine
The Atomic Ballerina
A Haunt of Jackals
The Gallows of Heaven

Fallen Rogues
A city of rogues. A seedy bar. A thief who stole the wrong prize.

The Midnight Monster Club
The Dragon and Rose
The Chapel of the Wyrm
The Isle of the Fallen

www.ingramcontent.com/pod-product-compliance
Lightning Source LLC
Chambersburg PA
CBHW072131300726
48975CB00003B/1014